INEVITABLE
CIRCUMSTANCES

INEVITABLE
CIRCUMSTANCES

S.R. GREY

Inevitable Circumstances (Inevitability #2)

Copyright © 2015 by S.R. Grey

ISBN-10: 0986156531 (print version)

ISBN-13: 978-0-9861565-3-3 (print version)

Editing: Hot Tree Editing

Cover Design: Arijana Karčić, Cover It! Designs

Interior Formatting: E.M. Tippetts Book Designs

Books by
S.R. GREY

A Harbour Falls Mystery trilogy

Harbour Falls
Willow Point
Wickingham Way

Judge Me Not trilogy

I Stand Before You
Never Doubt Me
Just Let Me Love You

Inevitability duology

Inevitable Detour
Inevitable Circumstances

Laid Bare novella series
Exposed: Laid Bare 1
Unveiled: Laid Bare 2 (June 2015)
Spellbound: Laid Bare 3 (August 2015)

PROLOGUE

Essa

After Farren, Haven, and I arrive in New York City, I keep waiting for the ax to fall, for Farren to be pulled away from me. I fear Dawson, and I loathe the thought of Farren leaving to go hunt him down. But I know Dawson and his organization must be stopped. If not, we will always be in danger.

As Farren helps Haven and I settle into his spacious, luxurious apartment—one with an amazing view of Central Park—my worries are temporarily assuaged. Farren's business partner, Rick Martinez, and Vincent, the undercover FBI agent, both of who remain in New Mexico, are unable to pinpoint a location for Dawson.

Farren gets to stay, for now. *Yay!*

He tells me, "Let's make the most of it, Essa." And we do.

Farren shows me and Haven around the city, and our first two weeks are spent sightseeing, going to museums, and eating in a variety of restaurants. We even take in a couple of shows. Haven, the wannabe actress, loves those nights most of all.

When Farren and I are alone we stroll over to Central Park. We walk and we talk. Sometimes we pack a picnic lunch and eat in Sheep Meadow. And every day I fall more in love with Farren.

He loves me, as well. Apart from telling me often, love shines in his emerald eyes.

Haven, who recovers day-to-day from her traumatic experience, becomes more and more interested in Rick. He definitely like her, too. They speak whenever they can and text often. She tells me he plans to spend some time in New York City, once the situation with Dawson is resolved.

Haven also stays in contact with her father, and Mr. Barnes again invites her to his mansion in Connecticut. She politely informs him she's still not ready. To me, she confides that there are many things weighing on her mind, like deciding where she wants to finish her degree—in Pennsylvania or here in New York. When Farren gets word she may return to Oakwood College, he abruptly takes off one afternoon, on what he terms "personal business."

The next day, a friend of mine and Haven's calls to let us know Professor Walsh has resigned for no apparent reason. *Good riddance*, I think.

That night, in bed, I ask Farren, "Was that your doing?"

Farren never lies to me, not after all we've been through, and this night is no exception. He turns to his side and, facing me, says, "That asshole fucking broke my sister's heart. If she decides to go back to that school, I don't want him anywhere near her."

Not that I am concerned for Asshole Walsh, but I do have to ask, "You didn't, um, hurt him, did you?"

Farren laughs and rolls to his back. Staring up at the ceiling, still chuckling, he says, "No, Essa. I didn't have to *hurt* him. He was easy to persuade."

"Well, for the record," I say softly, "I'm glad he's out of Oakwood. For Haven's sake, if she does decide to return. But also for the other girls he took advantage of."

"Hmm…" Farren murmurs.

I don't ask him for specifics of how he "persuaded" the prick to quit. It doesn't matter. Some things are best left unknown.

Farren peers over at me curiously, and, after a minute, I say, "What?"

"Just wondering what *your* decision is going to be." Brushing my blonde locks over my shoulder, he continues. "Are you going back to Oakwood in the fall, or are you staying here?"

Farren already informed me that with a few phone calls—from him and also, not surprisingly, his influential father—I can attend Columbia this fall, if I want. Farren doesn't know I made my decision a while ago, and without further ado, I tell him. "I decided, Farren. I'm staying."

Thrilled, he scoops me up and settles me on top of his hard body. Winding his hand through my hair, he pulls me down, bringing me closer to his face.

"Kiss me, Essa," Farren huskily demands.

Only too happy to oblige my gorgeous boyfriend, I kiss him with fervor. He kisses me back intensely. Farren kisses with heart, soul, and finesse, making me gasp when we finally stop.

When I've caught my breath, I say, "Wow. Guess you like my decision."

"You think?" he teases in a sultry tone.

His hands travel down my back till he's cupping my ass. I

wiggle into place, straddling him, and as always, he's up and ready.

When I mention this observation to him, he laughs. "I am a soldier, Essa. Therefore, I am *always* prepared for action on a moment's notice."

"Hey!" I smack his shoulder. "You're supposed to say you're always like this"—I press my core to his rock-hard sex—"because of me."

In a more serious tone, he says, "My reaction is because of you, Essa."

Sighing, I tell him, "I love you, Farren."

"I love you, too, sweetheart," he replies.

I start to rub my body back and forth, but he stills me with a hand to my hip. "Wait," he says.

I feel him throbbing—as am I—so I ask, "Why? What's wrong?"

He chuckles, and I know from the timbre of his voice that he wants full control, typical alpha-male that he is. Sure enough, he slides into me unrepentantly, eliciting a throaty moan from me.

"Nothing is wrong, Essa. Everything"—he thrusts up into me, and I gasp—"is absolutely perfect."

Yeah, everything is perfect. Our love is solid.

The following day I meet with a career-services counselor at Columbia. She hammers out a schedule guaranteeing I'll graduate in three semesters. It puts me a little behind the eight ball, but I'll come out with a major in journalism and a minor in business. Not too shabby.

When I return to the apartment, anxious to share my news with Farren, I find him whipping up dinner in the kitchen. He's hot and adorable in dark dress pants, a white button-down shirt with the sleeves rolled up, and an apron with a rooster on the front. The printed message beneath the rooster reads, "Kiss the Cock."

"I don't think Haven will appreciate your humor," I say, nodding to the apron.

"What?" He looks down, all innocent. "It's a reference to the chicken."

"Yeah," I reply, laughing, "sure it is."

He looks over at the clock on the wall. "Damn," he mutters.

"What?"

"Haven will be home soon. I was hoping if we had more time, you could show me what you think the message on the apron means."

He looks so delicious that I definitely would not mind showing him. But it's true that Haven will be back soon, so I sigh and raise a brow. "Later?"

"Most definitely later," he replies with a smile that melts me. He adjusts himself discreetly and then returns to chopping up some green peppers.

"So," he begins after a beat, "how'd it go today at Columbia?"

"Surprisingly well." I grab a piece of green pepper, crunch into it, and give Farren the details, adding at the end, "I think the business minor will keep my parents happy."

Chuckling, he asks, "Yeah, but what do you think they'll say about your living arrangements?"

I plan on staying at Farren's apartment.

"I'm twenty-two," I state, "an adult. I can live wherever the hell I want."

With an assessing look, Farren stops chopping peppers. Slowly, he says, "You've changed a lot, Essa."

"I have," I agree. And, a little while later, I discover my parents have changed some as well. When I declare my intentions for my future—living arrangements, change of school, and all—they react well, accepting my decision.

The newly assertive me can be persuasive, I suppose. My parents don't even cut me off financially. Still, if I'm to be an adult, I know it's time to start earning some money of my own.

I resolve to find a job for the summer. Haven is signed up for an acting workshop that meets every weekday morning, and Farren has frequent meetings with his father. I need something to do, too.

There's still no sign of Dawson, but I know it's only a matter of time. A job will keep me occupied, and it will keep me busy when Farren has to leave. So, on one particularly bright and sunny summer afternoon, I apply at the coffee shop around the corner from the apartment.

"I'm not crazy about you working there," Farren says later in the day, when I tell him of my new employment.

"Why?" I inquire, baffled.

He shrugs. "I don't know. I don't have a specific reason." Sighing, he then admits, "I guess I just want to keep you protected at all times." Farren is not immune to worrying about me, same as I worry for him.

I wrap my arms around him. "I like when you're protective," I assure him. "But trust me, I'll be fine." When he huffs, I remind him, "The coffee shop is, like, two minutes from here."

"I know." He nestles me closer to his strong body. "Just be careful, Essa. Don't trust anyone."

Three days into my new employment Mr. Barnes asks Farren to accompany him on a business trip to a third-world country.

His father wants his son there not only for protection, but also as a consultant.

I begin to get the impression Farren's father fully intends to leave his empire to his remaining children at some point. I think that's why he keeps trying so hard to connect with Haven.

Before Farren leaves, it's my turn to ask him to be careful. In a sad voice, I add, "I'm going to miss you so much."

"I'll only be gone two weeks," Farren replies in a conciliatory tone.

"Still…" I trail off.

He knows this will be hard because we've been together almost every day for more than two months. Enfolding me in his arms, he softly murmurs, "I'll miss you, too, Essalin."

And then he leaves.

With Farren gone, I decide to fully immerse myself in my coffee-shop job. I spend time getting to know the other employees. I ask them about their kids, their spouses, their lives. I get to know all the regular customers, too, and most of them are pretty cool.

One particular guy catches my eye. Not in a romantic way, of course, it's just that my heart goes out to him. He's around my age, a college student. At least, that's what I gather, since he trundles in every morning with a passel of textbooks. The guy is kind of cute, in a nerdy, klutzy kind of way. He wears glasses and has a mop of reddish hair, but it works for him. He gets noticed by women in the shop, but he only talks to me. I guess that's because I am infinitely patient with him. Like, when his books slip from his grasp, I help him adjust them before they fall. When he drops his money on the counter, I pick it up. And when he almost knocks over his usual order—iced coffee—I catch it before it topples.

Our conversations are a series of him saying, "I'm so sorry... Oh, let me get that... Shit."

My responses are: "Don't worry about it... I got it... You're good."

One morning, before walking away, but after paying, this clumsy guy squints at me, eyeing my nametag.

"Essa," he says, his eyes scanning up to my face, soulful brown eyes hidden behind glasses. "I'm Justin, by the way."

"Nice to meet you, Justin," I say, and then I shake his hand.

And so it goes.

On the day Farren is set to return from his trip, I wrap up my morning shift a few minutes early. Klutzy, red-haired Justin walks to the door just as I do. I notice he's completely distracted, though, peering down at a paperback in one hand, wrapped up in reading. An iced coffee is in his other hand, held way out in front of him, almost like he's trying to clear the way...to me.

Customers step left and right, avoiding the distracted Justin, but it's too late for me. My fiery-headed friend crashes right into me, and iced coffee splatters down the front of my green work shirt.

Looking aghast, he says, "Oh, hell, Essa. I didn't see you there." He puts his paperback down on a nearby table and starts reaching for napkins from a dispenser. "I'm so, so sorry."

"Oh, don't worry about it." I take the napkins from him and start dabbing, however, recycled paper material is no match for the soaking I've received. When it's clear the napkins are not helping, I say, "I think I better go clean up in the ladies' room."

"Wait," Justin says, his voice sounding suddenly urgent. "My car is parked around the corner. I have some auto-detailing towels in there. They're very absorbent."

I shrug. "Okay, sure. Let's try those."

As we're walking to Justin's car, I take a stab at making conversation. "So, you keep a car in New York City. That's kind of crazy."

"I know, right." He laughs. "It would be, too. But I don't live in the city."

"Oh, where do you live?" I ask as we turn into an alley used mainly for morning deliveries.

"Jersey," he says just as we reach his car. "Here it is." He gestures to the simple brown Toyota, a typical student car.

Justin reaches for the passenger-door handle, and I take a step closer. And that's when I notice there's someone seated in the passenger seat.

"Oh…" I start backing up.

Justin gets behind me, his moves suddenly swift and sure. "What the hell?" I mutter.

"Not so fast, Essa," this new, confident Justin says in my ear.

His voice is smooth, controlled. No more uncertain, nerdy college guy. Who is this guy? Clearly, Justin is not who I thought he was.

My heart begins to pound frantically as he nudges me closer and closer to his car. Within seconds I am trapped between the Toyota and Justin's body.

I have no choice but to look inside the car, and when I see who's sitting casually in the passenger seat, I gasp, "Shit. Dawson."

I try to spin around so I can flee, but Justin holds me firmly in place. I glance left and right. No one is around. I am so screwed.

Dawson pops open the door, making Justin and I move back a foot. And then the man I hoped to never lay eyes on again leans forward. Pinning me with cold, hard eyes, he says icily, "Ah, we meet again, young Essalin. I think I'd like to spend some time with you, much more time than our first meeting. Perhaps you should get in the car."

CHAPTER ONE

Farren

You would think a man might find solace thirty-five thousand feet above the cold, blue Atlantic. Or, you might think a man sitting in the plush interior of a private jet—with reduced cabin noise, no less—would perhaps lead to that man's peace, maybe some gentle reflection, even.

You might think these things, right?

Well, guess what? You'd be dead wrong.

See, the truth, for me, is a state of mind far, far away from any kind of solace, peace, or gentle reflection.

Not that I deserve any of those things. Fuck no. Not after the things I've done, including what I did the other day.

I blow out a breath, and we descend slightly, like the jet is as exasperated as I feel.

"Fuck," I murmur, scrubbing both hands down my face.

These hands—I glare down at them—they appear so normal.

Just an everyday man's hands, a little rough here and there, but overall clean and tidy. No one would guess the level of violence I've meted out with these babies. Not even Essa, *especially* not Essa.

A voice rings out, pulling me from my soul-searching reverie. "Are you okay, son?" Barnes asks, a reminder that I'm not alone in this plane.

Barnes lowers the iPad he's working on and swivels his plushy chair, across the spacious aisle, till he's facing me.

Then, he studies me.

I say, with more confidence that I feel, "I'm fine, okay?"

What does Quinton Barnes really see, though? A reflection of the man he used to see whenever he looked in the mirror, some thirty years ago. I have the same raven-black hair he once had. I have the same green eyes, too.

Does he see me in him? I hope not, I am my own man.

"Quit staring," I bite out, reaching for a glass of clear liquid on a small table in front of me. I take a drink, wishing it was vodka instead of water.

"I'm sorry, son," my father says, shifting uncomfortably. "I didn't mean to make you uncomfortable."

"No problem, *Dad*."

First time I've called Barnes that, and it feels kind of weird. But it's my olive branch, my apology for acting like a dick at this, the tail-end of our trip.

Barnes raises his brows, nods slowly, his approval of my recognizing he is who he is—my father. My father, who I thought was dead and gone, lost forever. But no, Barnes came back in to my life last year when his teenage daughter—a sister I never met, never knew I had—was kidnapped by human traffickers, and subsequently murdered.

Sounds crazy, right? It sure the hell is. Crazy, though, is par for the course for me. Nothing in my life is normal. Well, except for Essa. She gives my existence a sense of normalcy, something I desperately need.

Sighing, I can't help but think: *If she only knew the full truth. She'd take her normal self and run far, far away from me.*

"We'll be touching down in New York in less than an hour," Barnes says, attempting to make conversation with me…again.

He wants to chat. I can't blame him; it has been a long fucking flight.

"You'll probably be home in time for dinner," he continues. "That'll be nice, yes?"

"That will be great," I say, my tone clipped. I just don't feel like talking. "Thanks."

But my father continues. "Do you think Essa will be cooking up something special for your homecoming?"

I've been out of town for a couple of weeks, and during that time Essa has been trying her hand at cooking, or so she's told me during our many phone calls. I told Barnes this the other day, but I'm surprised he remembers. In any case, Essa may indeed have a homecoming meal in the works for me. Still, I don't feel like talking about my girlfriend with Barnes, not when I feel guilty enough for keeping secrets from her.

I give my father a one-shoulder shrug as my response, and Barnes gets the hint and goes back to messing with his iPad.

You're an asshole, Shaw, some inner voice whispers.

I'm not trying to be a dick, I swear I'm not. There's no reason for me to act this way, not with Barnes. He's done right by me. Not that I haven't done right by him in return. After all, it was me who gave him the honors of taking out that scumbag, Eric, the man who tortured and killed his daughter, Annemarie—the sister I never met.

Righteous vengeance, if I do say so myself.

Eric...that motherfucking... Even thinking about that tall fucking Swede gets my blood boiling. He deserved to die, and I don't feel bad he's gone. Not only did he have a hand in Annemarie's death, but he was also the man who orchestrated my sister's kidnapping. My other sister, that is. The sister I've known all my life and love dearly—Haven.

Haven would have ended up murdered, just like Annemarie, had Rick not gotten to her in time. Thankfully, though, under my direction, my business partner was able to whisk my sister away from Eric and his sordid associates.

But...there's still a bigger problem out there. The real leader of the human trafficking ring that took Haven and Annemarie is still alive and kicking.

Not for long if I have anything to say about it. Yeah, Dawson is my next target.

He needs to be put down before he gets to Essa. And he will, get to her that is. Hell, that fucking pig took too much of a liking to my girlfriend the day we met up with him at his compound in the desert. Essa thinks Dawson watching me get her off on the hood of a car was humiliating. If only she knew the things he'd do to her if he ever got her alone.

A shudder runs through me at the thought and Barnes glances over at me curiously.

"Something wrong?" he asks.

Lifting my hand, I wave him off. "It's nothing."

Barnes cocks a brow. "You sure, Farren?"

14

"Yes, I'm sure."

Truth is I have more on my mind than eliminating Dawson. After he's dealt with I need to sit down and decide how much of my "real" life I am going to reveal to Essa. She thinks this trip was just a matter of me going out of town on business with my father. And it was, for the most part.

It's what I was asked to do two days ago that haunts me this afternoon.

Sighing, I turn away from Barnes, and catching my reflection in the plane window, I realize I sure as hell don't look like the lethal man I am beneath the outer handsome-man facade. I know women are attracted to me. Essa tells me all the time how "hot" I am, how "delicious" my muscles are. She says I look like a man that can take care of business, in the bedroom…and out of it.

I chuckle at the thought.

Yeah, I take damn good care of every one of Essa's needs. She likes the feeling she gets when I am rough with her, the way I handle her, sexually, like I could break her in two. But I never would, of course.

Still doesn't mean I am anything close to safe. In truth, I am far more dangerous than Essa could ever imagine. I've killed men with my bare hands. In fact, I have the skill and ability to take out *any* living thing that gets in my way. I only use those skills when necessary, though…or when I'm called upon to use them.

And that brings me back to the other day.

There was a situation that needed to be taken care of in the third-world country Barnes happened to have business in. A highly placed government official, a man who had been on the U.S. administration's payroll at one time, had turned. As a result, he needed to be "dealt with."

And that's where I came in.

Barnes knows nothing of what I had to do. When I left our hotel room I told him I was going out to meet up with an old business associate. There was doubt in my dad's eyes, even as he nodded and said, "Okay."

My father is a very smart man, and I'm sure he knew right then that there was more to my departure.

After I left I picked up a car that had been arranged for me. In an alley filled with closed-up vendor kiosks, I checked over the sniper rifle that was in the trunk. And then I drove to where I was ordered to lie in wait.

Two hours later I took care of business, business Essa would never dream of. No, my life is sometimes the stuff of nightmares.

I hate lying to Essalin. We don't do that to each other. But no one can know what I do. Not even Rick Martinez, my work partner who's been with me for over a decade, knows the full truth. He suspects something, but he doesn't press. As far as the agency I work for views things, not only do *they* not exist, but neither do I. I am a ghost, a myth, a man who slips in unnoticed. I get shit done, and then I disappear.

Problem is, I *do* exist, especially when I'm around Essa. She's my touchstone, my key to retaining sanity in my messed-up world. When I touch Essalin, I feel normal. I feel more *real*. She reminds me of what's really important in life.

Turning away from my reflection, I lean back and close my eyes. *Fuck, I shouldn't care.* I am trained not to feel, not to reflect in this way. But falling for Essalin Brant has changed me.

I never saw her coming. Not in a million years did I expect to fall for someone, especially a college girl, same age as my sister. But, damn, if Essa didn't freight-train her ass right into my heart, and at the worst possible time, too. Starting something with her while my sister was in trouble was *never* my intention. I couldn't stop myself, though.

Flirting, making a move, I couldn't keep my fucking distance. *Damn.* Spending all those days and nights together, weeks on end, and under that kind of pressure, you could say things just happened. Hey, don't judge. You can't predict how you'll respond to grief. We are all different, and for me, grief left my heart open for connection. And all that time Essa was making me feel things I'd never before felt.

You can't fight motherfucking destiny. That is what I learned. That bitch will grab you by the balls and squeeze until you're writhing on the ground. Destiny, fate, stuff Essa likes to talk about, well, that shit always wins…even against me.

So I gave in, and wouldn't you know it, I motherfucking fell in love. I never meant for that to happen, men like me don't "do" love. Sure, I've dated, fucked quite a few along the way, but, truth is, I've never been a hearts and flowers kind of guy. For Essa, though, I'm willing to change. For us, I want that happy ending.

Dream on, my practical side whispers. *Once she knows all the shit you've done—the shit you still do—she will be so fucking done with you.*

That may be true. Essa *thinks* she knows what I do, but there is so much more to tell her. She knows about my Special Forces background, yes, but she doesn't know I'm still in it, only in a different capacity. I'm Black Ops now, with a secret agency. Not only that, but I'm in deep.

The reason I didn't storm in and rescue my sister from the bad guys was I'd been ordered *not* to. Too much risk of jeopardizing my identity, or so I was told. I had no choice but to order Rick to take over.

I guess that shit left me open to Essa, too. I needed some control in my life. Because of who I am—a top-level sniper—my decisions are often made by others. Time and again I am directed to ferret out the worst of the worst, and then, eliminate them. My actions are for the greater good of the world. I tell myself this all the time, but there's no getting around the fact that when it comes right down to it I am a killer.

So how am I supposed to peer in to Essa's naïve whiskey-colored eyes and tell her the truth about myself? How am I supposed to casually disclose to her all the things I've done, all the shit I've seen? And most disturbing of all is how the fuck do I tell the woman I love that only two days ago I killed a man in cold blood?

Fuck, will she ever forgive me?

CHAPTER TWO

Essa

H E has a gun. I see it in his lap. There's a silencer on it.

"Get in the car," Dawson says once more, this time with increased impatience.

He lifts the gun an inch, threatening, while Justin nudges me from behind. "Listen to him," he urges.

There's an edge of desperation in his voice, and he almost sounds like the guy I knew before this morning. Well, the guy I *thought* I knew. How well, though, can you really know someone who's just a customer at the coffee shop where you work?

Not very well at all, I surmise when Justin reaches behind me and pops open the back door on the passenger side.

There's no getting out of this situation I've gotten myself in to. Still, I hold my ground, remaining unmoving.

"Get in," Justin urges again, a little more insistently.

My pulse races, and, shit, I'm scared. No, this is beyond

frightened. I am terrified.

"I can't move," I whimper. "I mean, I really *can't* move, Justin."

And it's the truth. Whereas initially I was just behaving like a stubborn brat, I now literally can't move. My feet refuse to go.

Dawson growls, "If you don't get in this fucking car..." He leans out the front door menacingly. "I will shoot you in the fucking kneecap, Ms. Brant. Then, you'll have a real reason not to move."

"He's not kidding," Justin says, a hint of apology creeping into his voice.

I know Dawson is deadly serious, so I muster the strength and force one foot in front of the other. A not-so-gentle shove from Justin and I am catapulted into the backseat, head first.

Quickly, I scramble and right myself. As I settle back, something hard presses up against my ass cheek.

And then I remember. *Oh, my God, my cell phone is in the back pocket of my jeans.*

How could this be? Come to think of it, why has no one frisked me or patted me down? Maybe Justin was supposed to before we reached the car. He must have forgotten. Or maybe he was watching me in the café and didn't see when I slipped my cell in my pocket before I left. If he missed it, he would think I had nothing on me that could pose a threat. No phone equates to no contacting authorities for help.

I have a phone, I have a phone.

I'm excited, my hope renewed, but I can't imagine Dawson letting something like this go overlooked for too long. I fully expect him to check me at some point, for things like cells, probably before we leave.

I glance around, hands shaking. There's still no one in sight.

The alley is the kind of place that's busy in the morning, with deliveries and such, and then dies out for the rest of the day. If only a single person happened by, they'd notice how amiss we all look. Any distraction, even someone walking over to check on things, and I might be able to call 911.

I cross my fingers, both hands, and furtively glance left and right, searching for *any* signs of activity. Luckily, Dawson and Justin don't notice what I'm doing since they're too busy discussing something. It sounds heated. Damn, this would be a great time for someone to walk by. But, of course, that'd be too easy. The alley remains dead, and I accept I am on my own.

Slumped in the backseat, I watch as Justin leans in the open front door, murmuring something to Dawson. His hand remains at the top edge of the slightly open back door, the door closest to me.

Stay calm, remain focused.

I tune out my dire circumstances and tune in to Dawson and Justin's conversation, hoping to glean some detail that may help. I messed up by trusting Justin, but I make a quick vow that from here on out I will try to think of what Farren would do. And what he would expect *me* to do. Believe it or not, I learned a lot from our time together on the road. If only I'd put into action what I knew, I wouldn't be in this situation now.

Stupid me, I should never have trusted someone I didn't know. Farren warned me. In my defense, though, Justin seemed so harmless. And besides, I'm new at this crazy cat-and-mouse game Dawson seems to thrive on.

One thing I will forever keep in mind, though, is that you can never judge a book by its cover.

Dawson and Justin's voices remain low, and mostly incoherent, but when they become a bit more animated I catch words of an impending change of vehicles, a change that's to occur after we leave the alley.

"There will be a white box truck parked at 122nd and Riverside," Dawson says softly.

"That's right by the Grant Tomb memorial, right?" says Justin.

"Yes. We'll make the switch there."

With the two men distracted, I know now may be the only time to act. Since I can't escape, nor can I whip out my phone and call authorities, I resolve to do the next best thing—leave a clue for Farren.

I have no doubt he will come searching for me once he realizes I'm missing. He'll retrace my path from the coffee shop, and a clue left in this creepy alley will show him the exact spot where I was taken. From there, Farren can lift shoe prints, tire-track impressions, and who knows what else.

I begin racking my brain for what kind of clue to leave. I have no purse, since I didn't bring one to work today. I was in a damn hurry this morning and forgot it at home. I had my keys to the apartment with me, but after a quick check of my pockets, I find they're no longer in my possession.

Shit, I must have set them down on a table when I was trying to clean up the coffee Justin spilled on me. I have my phone, of course, but I can't leave *that* in the alley. Surely Justin or Dawson would notice if I dropped something that large outside the car. Not to mention, an opportunity could still arise in which to use it.

I ponder…

If there was just something from the phone I could leave behind. A part pf some sort, a…aha!

That's when it hits me—I remember the small charm I keep on my phone. Something so tiny would be easy to drop undetected outside the slightly-open back door. More importantly, the charm is something Farren will recognize.

A few weeks ago Haven gave me the pink jeweled piece of metal, a heart shape she plugged right into the headphone jack on my phone. "There, we match," she said, laughing as she plugged a matching red heart charm into her own phone.

If I pull the charm out while the men are distracted, drop it outside the door, the shiny pink heart should catch Farren's eye.

Glancing at said door, I note that it's open just enough for me to accomplish this one thing. Only problem is Justin's hand still rests along the top edge. If I bump the door, even slightly, it will surely attract his attention.

This is going to be tricky.

Nonetheless, I must find the courage to get this one thing done. My life may depend on it.

Suddenly, Justin glances back at me. Only for a few seconds, but still, I quickly avert my gaze. Can't have him figuring out what I'm up to.

Subtly, he shifts his body, blocking more of the door. Wow, he must think I'm planning an escape of some sort. Yeah, right. That would be crazy, seeing as Dawson is in possession of a gun I *know* he'll use on me.

Don't worry, I think. *Like I'd try that kind of maneuver and get shot in the back.*

No, the charm is my only hope.

Justin and Dawson's discussion, something about money owed to him and when Dawson will get it to him, becomes more heated.

It's time to make my move.

Slowly, oh-so-slowly, I reach back to my pocket. Fine beads of perspiration form on my brow, fear of discovery and reprisal making me sweat. I sure as hell don't want to alert the men that I not only have a phone in my possession, but that I also have what I intend to leave as a clue for Farren.

If Dawson discovers what I'm up to, he will grant me no mercy. In fact, he'll probably use the opportunity to immediately commence with whatever horrific plans he has in store for me.

I shudder at the thought, but pull myself together quickly, knowing the men will only remain preoccupied for so long.

Finally, despite experiencing a level of fear I never knew possible, I tug the charm from the jack on my phone.

Step one, done. Take a breath.

Casually, I move my hand toward my lap, charm in hand, and then discreetly drop the tiny piece of metal just outside the door.

There's a tiny "tink" noise, and time stops.

The two men go silent.

I hold my breath.

One single glance is sent back my way, from Dawson, but it only lasts a beat. And then the men continue talking.

I'm safe. No one has noticed a thing. *Mission accomplished.*

My fear returns, though, when Justin mumbles something indecipherable and Dawson focuses back on me. Twisting around in the front seat, eyeing me up intently, his lips curve up into a sickly smile.

Gruffly, he says, "What are you up to back there, little one? You're awfully quiet."

"I'm not up to anything," I squeak out, hoping he can't hear the deception in my voice.

Be calm, that's how Farren would play it.

Dawson frowns, the lines deepening in his leathery, tanned face, making him appear crueler than ever.

"Did you frisk her?" he barks to Justin.

"Uh…" Justin trails off and shifts nervously from one foot to the other.

Suddenly, Dawson explodes. But his anger is not directed at Justin, the dude who forgot to frisk me. No, Dawson's fury is for some reason directed at me.

He yells, "Get out of the car, you little bitch! Right now, move!"

I freeze.

The backseat is definitely preferable to whatever Dawson plans to do to me outside the car. I waffle between obeying him, or not. But my decision is made for me, as I suspect all decisions will be made for me from here on out, when, with frighteningly fast speed for a man in his early sixties, Dawson jumps out and reaches into the back of the car. He promptly yanks me out, and I whimper.

Dawson smashes my body, face-first, up against the side of the car. In my ear, he growls, "Shut up, or else."

His fetid breath fills my nose, and I almost gag in response. I want to scream for help, anything, but the gun is pressed firmly to my side. I know this man will use it, too, if not to shoot me, then to pistol-whip me. Consequently, I refrain from uttering a peep.

The string of hope I've been holding onto begins to unravel, especially when Dawson twists my arm behind my back and crushes me to the side of the car.

"Ouch," I cry out, wincing.

"Let's see what you're hiding," Dawson says, unaffected by my pain. In fact, he seems to be enjoying it. He chuckles when his hands roam all over me, mostly in places where nothing could possibly be hidden. *Sick perv.*

In a whisper, I beg, "Please, stop."

He tightens his hold, twisting my arm so far behind my back it feels as if it may break in two.

Why is it that it's so hard to breathe when you're in pain? I wonder, trying to keep my rising panic at bay.

Gasping for air, I choke out, "Stop, stop, stop, please stop. You're hurting me."

"Hurting you?" Dawson laughs. "You don't know pain, bitch. But you will, oh, will you ever...unless you're willing to see reason, of course."

I don't know what his cryptic comment means, and I don't care. I don't know anything anymore. I start to cry, and Dawson spends extra time patting down my ass. When he comes to the bump in my back pocket, he, of course, discovers the phone.

The laughing and chuckling stops, but the resulting silence is worse.

"I can explain," I mumble.

He hits the back of my head. "Shut up."

Finally, he releases my arm from his grip. My poor arm, every muscle and tendon screaming out in pain. Before I have a chance to gather my senses, Dawson spins me around, and then smacks me across the face with an open hand.

My teeth graze across my bottom lip, and I start to bleed. Tears and blood, salt and copper, I am reduced to basic elements.

While I swipe dazedly at the blood on my lip, Dawson shoves me into the backseat.

"Don't move," he says.

I nod an assent as my lip swells, another injury to add to my aching arm.

Dawson is done with me, thank God, but he promptly starts in on Justin.

"Miss something like that next time," he warns as he pockets my phone, "and you're done."

"Yes, sir," Justin replies meekly. "I'm sorry, sir. I'll do better from here on out, I promise."

I realize then that Justin is just a kid, a young man, not a criminal. He may even truly be a student. Knowing Dawson, he probably recruited him, using the lure of cold, hard cash.

But, Jesus, how much money is worth involving yourself in this mess?

If Justin is having second thoughts, it's too late, for both of us. I am trapped, and he is stuck helping my captor.

While Dawson slides his trim body back into the front seat, I glance up at the red head looking down at the ground. How committed is he? Did he know Dawson planned to take it this far, that he always intended on kidnapping me?

Justin looks up, our eyes meeting briefly. He slams the back door swiftly, ending our contact. Huffing, he walks to the other side of the car.

Odd as it is, hope resurfaces. Why? One simple reason: in that brief exchange before Justin slammed the door I saw something in his brown eyes, something behind those nerdy glasses, and it's enough to lead me to believe Justin missed the phone in my pocket on purpose.

Not to get me—or himself—in trouble, but to give me a chance.

So, yeah, Justin may be my way out, he may be the weak link in Dawson's sinister plan.

I relax, ever so slightly. Between Justin's possible lack of commitment and Farren finding the charm I dropped on the ground, there is hope I will survive whatever comes next.

But it's the "whatever comes next" that makes me shudder.

CHAPTER THREE

Farren

AN hour after Barnes' private jet touches down on US soil, I arrive at my apartment. When I walk in and can't detect any aromas that would indicate cooking was taking place, I have to laugh.

"Aah, Barnes, you were so wrong," I say out loud, chuckling. Alas, there is no homecoming meal awaiting me.

I smile, imaging Essa trying earlier in the day to whip up something. She probably got frustrated and gave up. My smile turns into a low laugh, but then my amusement fades when I realize Essa is not even home. Worse yet, things feel…off. Nothing is blatantly amiss in the apartment, except it is eerily quiet in here. And a vague, general feeling of unease is coming over me, one I can't shake off.

Call it a sixth sense, if you will. Some people would say that's what it was. Whatever the fuck it is, I can tell you that that sixth sense has saved my life too many times to count. Unfortunately for my targets, it's that same uncanny perception that makes me a formidable sniper.

Walking slowly from room to room, I check around for anything unusual. Apart from the apartment being empty, everything else seems to be in place. Nothing untoward occurred in this location.

Sighing and chastising myself for overreacting, I head to the master bedroom to drop off the bag still hanging off my shoulder.

I'm not the kind of guy to assume things, so I'm fine with the fact that there is no special welcome-home dinner on the table. However, I'd be lying if I didn't admit I had hoped to find Essa at least waiting for me. Truth is I've missed her quite a lot. I want her back in my arms as soon as possible. Just one languorous kiss, and a few minutes of holding her close, would do me a world of good right now.

After I drop my bag on the bedroom floor, a chord of worry strums within me once again. I tamp it down and go to the kitchen, telling myself the whole way that I'm just wired from the mission I completed.

"This is New York, asshole, not some third-world hellhole. Essa and Haven are probably out having fun. So, settle your ass down," I murmur as I grab a cold beer from the fridge.

In the living room I turn on a plasma TV mounted on the wall and plop down on the black leather sofa. Just as I'm hunkering down for a quiet evening ahead, the front door flies open.

"Farren, Farren are you home?" Haven is calling out frantically. "Oh, please be home. Farren, if you're here, I need to talk to you. It's important."

My sister is panicked about something, so I lean forward, set my beer on the glass surface of the coffee table, and yell back, "I'm in here, Hav, in the living room."

Haven appears in the doorway not two seconds later. She pauses, leaning on the doorframe for support. "Oh, thank God," she exclaims, breathless. "I was hoping and praying you were back from your trip."

Standing swiftly—something is definitely wrong—I go to her. "Are you okay?" I ask, checking her over. "What's going on? Did something happen?"

"Oh, Farren…" She trails off, hanging her head, her raven hair a veil around her clearly distressed face.

My sister isn't prone to panic. In fact, she's quite the opposite. Haven is resilient and strong. She's stoic in many ways, but standing here now she appears as if she may either start crying or crumple to the floor.

Turning her to face me fully, I place my hands on her elbows, steadying her. "Hey, hey," I say as soothingly as I can. "You're scaring me here. Did something bad happen?"

My immediate concern is that an event of some sort has triggered a flashback, something from Haven's time in captivity. But then I sense that there's more to it than that.

"Fuck," I mutter, fearing the worst has occurred—Dawson has gotten to her.

"You didn't see Dawson somewhere here in the city, did you?" I carefully ask.

"No, no." Haven shakes her head vociferously. "It's nothing like that."

She starts to shake, just a tremor, and I press, "Talk to me, Hav."

If Dawson hasn't approached my sister, he may have had

someone else do his dirty work for him. I know that man's fucking modus operandi and that's just his style.

"There haven't been any incidents with any strangers, have there?" I query.

I highly suspect Dawson will employ such a tactic—hire an innocuous-appearing individual, probably a guy or girl in their early twenties, to lure Haven or Essa into a trap. That's why I warned Essa not to trust *anyone* in New York. It's also the reason I still have reservations about her damn coffee-shop job.

Haven breathes in and out slowly, calming herself. "No one has approached *me*," she says. "But, Farren..." She trails off, looks away.

"Essa," I whisper, and Haven chokes back a sob.

Slowly, I step away. Not wanting to believe the unthinkable has happened, I say tersely, "Where is Essa, Haven?"

"I don't know," she says. "That's the problem, Farren. I can't find her anywhere."

"What do you mean you can't find her anywhere? Where in the hell is she?"

It's a fight to remain calm. I'm a pro at keeping my emotions under control, except when it comes to the woman I love.

In the calmest voice I can muster, I slowly inquire, "Did you check at the coffee shop? Essa worked an early shift, right? Maybe she stayed for a double. You know, make a little extra money for the summer."

Even as I say the words, I know they are not true. Essa knew I was coming home today; she never would have signed up for a double shift. But I, of all people, know denial is the first response when you know you are well and truly fucked.

And if Essa has been abducted, I am beyond fucked.

I watch as my sister exhales heavily. "Essa didn't work a double," she says, as I suspected she would. But then, to my surprise, she adds, "I went to the coffee shop to check on her, and I, uh, found out some…disturbing things." Her eyes, pained aquamarine, meet mine. "Farren, it doesn't look good."

Disturbing things, it doesn't look good, these words resonate in my head. I tense, ready to spring to action. I'm a do-er, not a talker. I want to go to the coffee shop immediately, interrogate witnesses who may be able to attest to Essa's last known movements. *I need to fucking find out what happened to my girlfriend!*

But first, I should hear Haven out.

She glances up at me, biting her lip as she tries to figure out how I'm handling this news.

Not well, my expression conveys.

She reaches out and touches my forearm. "Farren…"

"What did you find out?" I murmur, raking a hand through my hair.

Haven is smart, and I know her information will prove helpful. Pulling herself together—it's her turn to be strong for me, if only for a short while—she gives me the facts she's uncovered, all in a timeline fashion.

"I went to the coffee shop around noon," she begins. "My acting workshop wrapped up early, and I was thinking maybe Essa and I could catch a matinee movie. I knew she'd want to be back in time to see you"—we share a sad smile—"so I checked the run times of what's out so I'd have an idea of what to suggest."

"What happened when you first arrived at the coffee shop?"

Haven averts her eyes. "Essa wasn't there," she murmurs. "Uh, I asked to talk to the manager, and he said she left on time, right after her shift ended."

"Okay," I say, strained.

"There were a few weird things, though."

Her eyes meet mine, then she looks away.

"Like what?" I press.

"Well, first, Essa's apartment keys were lying on one of the tables. It was like she'd set them down for a second, but then forgot to pick them back up."

Haven and I share another look, this time for a meaningful several seconds. If Essa left her keys at the coffee shop and never came back for them, it means something happened right afterward. She never made it back to the apartment.

"Fuck." I bite out. "This isn't looking good."

"I tried to get more from the manager," Haven says in a rush, like maybe if she gets it all out we can solve the mystery of *where-is-Essa* right now. "He didn't have anything helpful, though. So, I started asking around. An employee named Kelly who was working all day had some good info."

I'm proud of my sister's fast thinking. "Good thinking, Hav," I tell her, "Did this Kelly have any idea of where Essa might have gone?"

My sister takes a breath, like she's gearing up to hit me with something I absolutely will not like. She leans back on the doorframe, and says, "Apparently, Essa left with a customer, a regular that's in there a lot. Some guy named Justin. According to Kelly, he only talks with Essa. He's a college student and—"

"Whoa, wait up a sec." I'm stumped, and a little irritated, as well. "Essa never mentioned any college student to me."

Turning away from my sister, I start to pace around the living room. I need to think this thing through before I jump to conclusions.

"I've talked with Essalin a lot these past couple of weeks, Hav, and she never once mentioned a guy named Justin from the coffee shop."

I can't help it, a pang of jealousy hits me in the heart. I knock that shit down, though, since something more sinister than some random dude hitting on my girl while she's at work is at play here.

"She never mentioned him to me, either," Haven says, sounding wounded.

I know Haven and Essa share a lot, and I have to wonder why Essa would keep this guy a secret. I can come up with one reason only—Essa knew I'd disapprove.

"Essa is fucking naïve to the ways of the world," I bite out.

I'm angry at Essa, but far angrier when I play out what probably happened. I'm certain this Justin dude is somehow involved in why Essa is not here at the apartment, safe and happy with me and my sister.

"I need to go to the coffee shop," I say.

I start to brush past Haven, but she grabs my arm, stopping me cold. "Wait," she pleads. "I want to come with you."

"Haven, I don't think that's a good idea." Turning to my sister, I smile sadly as I tuck a strand of hair the color of mine behind her ear. "I know you want to help, but I really need for you to stay at the apartment. I can't have you going missing, too, right?" I don't wait for an answer. "Listen, this is the safest place for you to be right now. Okay?"

She nods and acquiesces. "Okay, Farren."

Haven is worried; it's written all over her face. She's thinking the same thing as I am—this supposed college kid was a plant by Dawson.

"Keep your phone handy," I tell her. "I'll call as soon as I know anything."

Haven nods again, only this time there are tears in her eyes. "Farren," she chokes out. "I'm scared. I'm scared for Essa, I'm scared for you, and I'm scared for me."

She starts to shake, and I wrap my arms around her still-so-frail frame.

My sister went through a horrific ordeal two months ago. It's nothing short of amazing how well she's recovered. She's resilient, though, like me. Resiliency is a Shaw family trait. We didn't have a traditional upbringing, and our responses to terrible things aren't the same as how other people might react. When bad things happen, we deal, and then we move on. It's how we Shaws' roll. However, there are times, like these, when Haven's emotional scars bubble to the surface.

She starts to cry, and I try my best to comfort her. "Hey, hey,"—I tighten my arms around her tiny form—"nothing bad is going to happen to you. And Essa will be fine. You know I'll find her."

"Will you?" Haven sobs on my shoulder, her tears soaking the black T-shirt I'm wearing.

I step back and look down at her. I need to make her laugh; she doesn't need this kind of stress. "Do you really doubt my abilities, Hav?" I cover my heart with my hand, feigning wounded. "That hurts, you know."

That gets her to smile. "No, I guess I know you'll find her."

I pretend to be aghast. "You *guess*?"

"Farren"—she smacks my chest—"stop it. I know you're more than capable of finding Essa."

I look into her eyes and see blatant fear. And that shit hurts.

In a much more serious tone, I add, "Don't be afraid, okay?

You're here in New York with me. Nothing bad is going to happen to you in this apartment. I can guarantee that."

It's the truth. Even when I'm not here, my place is under constant surveillance, courtesy of our fine government protecting their valuable asset—me.

She raises a brow. "What about when I'm out?"

"I've done everything I can to keep you safe, but I can't stop you from living your life. Not that I would even want to do that, Haven. But know that, like what happened with Eric, if anyone ever tries to hurt you, they will have to answer to me. It's the same for Essa. You know this, right?"

"I do," she says. "That's why you let our father kill Eric. It wasn't just for what he did to Annemarie, was it?"

"No, it wasn't. It was for what he did to you, too."

"Would you have killed Eric if Barnes couldn't have done it?"

"Yes, in a heartbeat."

Haven pauses, and then asks, "Would you kill for Essa, too… if it came down to that?"

"Yes, you know I would."

She eyes me curiously, knowing me as only a sibling can. "What do you really do, Farren? I know you do more than work with Rick."

I shake my head. "Haven, you know I can't—"

Waving her hand, she says, "Never mind. Forget I asked."

I have to remain silent. I can't tell her what I really do, either.

Suddenly, Haven covers her face with her hands. "Oh, Farren," she mumbles through her fingers. "This is so bad. If Dawson has Essa, how will you ever find her? He's far more cunning than Eric, more dangerous, more, just, *everything.*"

I reach out, lowering her hands from her face. "Haven, *I* am far more cunning and dangerous than Eric *or* Dawson." I blow out a breath. "I am the most lethal of them all." I wish I could tell her more, alleviate her panic, but the best I can do is say, "No one can hide from me forever. If Dawson has Essa, I *will* find them. And I will kill him, either before or after I bring Essa back."

Haven gives me a small, hopeful smile, and I can't bring myself to add that I just hope to God I can bring Essa back alive.

A T the coffee shop, around the corner from my apartment, I explain who I am and what my relationship is to Essa. I give all this info to a manager who listens intently, but looks like he belongs on the beach serving ice cream instead of coffee. With apology in his youthful blue eyes, he gestures to a table. "We should sit," he says.

"Sure."

I'm fine with standing, but if sitting down results in this kid relaxing, and possibly remembering an important detail, I am onboard with that.

So we sit.

And the manager's story remains the same: Essa finished her shift on time, with nothing out of the ordinary occurring, and then she left.

"Oh," the manager adds, like an afterthought. "Essa did leave the store with a stranger. I guess that qualifies as unusual."

I resist the urge to sarcastically retort, "You think?"

He says, "Kelly, one of our employees, actually saw everything. I didn't know any of this earlier, not until after she talked to your sister." He stands, the chair scraping the floor. "Uh, I can go get her now, if you'd like."

Rubbing my temple, I sigh. "Yeah, that'd be great."

Three minutes later, Kelly emerges from the back. She's wiping her hands on her khaki pants. When she approaches the table I'm seated at, it's with trepidation. I give her my most charming smile to hopefully relax her.

"Mr. Shaw?" she says, smiling back as she offers her hand.

I have a good decade on the girl, but there's no need for formalities. Taking her hand, I give a firm shake, and say, "Just Farren is fine."

"Okay, Mr. Shaw. I mean Farren."

She smiles thinly as she takes a seat across from me. Hot pink streaks in her dark hair shimmer under the harsh artificial lights. She glances up at the lights, then to the door, then back at me. "You okay?" I ask.

"Yes." She nods. "Just nervous."

"Don't be." Another charming smile, this one working.

"All right." She smiles back at me.

And then I get down to business. "Thanks for talking with me, Kelly. I really appreciate it."

"Sure," she replies. "It's not a problem. I want to help."

"Are you ready, then?"

"Yes." She places her hands on the table, and I notice her nail color matches the streaks in her hair. "Where should I start?"

Right to the point, I ask, "Who is the guy Essa left with? Do you know him?"

"Not really," she says. "I only know his name is Justin. I overheard him talking one day. He was introducing himself to Essa."

"And this same guy, this Justin, he interacted with Essa this morning?"

"Yes." Kelly takes a deep breath. "He spilled something on her, iced coffee, I guess. Essa was standing in front of him, over by the entrance." She gestures with one hand to the door. "She was trying to wipe her shirt with a bunch of napkins before they went outside."

"Essa was still in her work clothes, then?"

"Yes, jeans and"—she points to her own green polo-style shirt—"a top like this."

I lean back in my chair. "Anything else I need to know?"

Kelly shakes her head. "No, I don't think so... Oh wait, there is one thing."

I raise a questioning brow.

"Uh, it's just that Justin is a regular, like, nowadays only. He never came in before Essa started working here."

"Hmmm." I don't like the sound of that or the implications. "Regarding Justin," I continue, "can you give me a description?"

Eyeing me with sudden suspicion, Kelly says, "Are you really just a concerned boyfriend?"

"Yes. Why would you think anything else?"

She shrugs. "I don't know. You ask questions like you've done this before. You sure you're not a cop?"

Chuckling, I assure her, "No, I'm not a cop." I smile reassuringly. "I'm just a concerned boyfriend who is worried and wondering where his girlfriend wandered off to."

"That's sweet," she says, blushing.

Now her cheeks match her hair and her nails. We're three for three here.

With doe-eyes directed my way, she gushes, "Wow, you know what? Essa is one lucky girl to have someone like you for a boyfriend. Protective, you know, caring. Just"—she shrugs—

"wow."

I continue to smile, but all I can think is this: *I failed my girl. My protectiveness was for shit when I was halfway around the globe.*

In a solemn tone more fitting for the circumstances, the girl gives me a pretty good description of the mysterious Justin—reddish hair, glasses, tall and lanky. "Kind of nerdy," she adds, "and really klutzy, too."

"Klutzy?" I can't imagine Dawson hiring someone inept, so I'm sure Justin's clumsiness was all an act.

"Yeah," she says, "he drops things all the time. Like, he always has his textbooks with him, and they're forever slipping from his hands. Stuff like that."

"Textbooks, huh? Is he a student at a local college?"

She shrugs. "I don't know. I would think so."

"Can you tell me anything more about him? Do you have a last name for this guy? Do you know where he lives, or what kind of car he drives?"

Already, before my questions are barely out, Kelly is shaking her head. "No. I am so sorry, Farren, but I don't know anything more than what I've told you."

With the need to wrap up weighing on me—I want to check around outside before it's too dark—I thank Kelly with the pink-streaked hair. I tell her, "You were great. You had a lot of useful info."

She brightens. "Really?"

"Yes, really."

I expect her to get up and leave, but she remains seated. "Um," she says slowly. "Is Essa going to be okay? That guy, Justin, I realize you don't know him, but you don't think he would hurt her or anything, right? I mean, he seems so safe and all, what with him being so clumsy."

Exactly his intent, I think. But I don't want to upset the girl, so I simply say, "No, no, I'm sure it's nothing like that."

She frowns. "I hope I didn't give you the wrong impression, either."

"About what?"

"Well, I know you're worried as to where Justin and Essa may have gone off together, but if you're thinking Essa is cheating on you—"

That is so preposterous that I have to cut her off. "No, I don't think anything like that, not at all." At this point, and with what is possibly happening to Essa, I hate to even think it, but cheating wouldn't be so bad.

What a fucked-up life I lead.

Kelly finally stands. "Well, I better get back to work," she says, giving me a smile so genuine it hurts my heart a little. "Don't worry, Farren. I'm sure Essa is around and will be back in no time. Knowing her, she probably went off with Justin to help him with something. He's the needy type, like I said. And, well, you know how Essa is. She's sweet and good, you know?"

The girl smiles and I can't help but smile in return, a genuine smile myself this time, despite the dire circumstances. "Yes," I quietly agree, "Essa is sweet and good like that."

It's true. Essa's sweetness and goodness are two of the things I love the most about her.

Unfortunately, I fear the same two traits may have led to her undoing earlier today.

CHAPTER FOUR

Essa

THE glimmer of hope I was feeling earlier begins to fade, just as the warm summer day turns to an unseasonably chilly night. *How fitting for my circumstances*, I think. A day that started out bright and full of possibility has turned hopeless and cold.

After the vehicle switch—car to box truck at the designated spot in Harlem—I am forced by Dawson and Justin to climb up into a dark, empty truck interior. It smells of metal and wood and, to me, hopeless desperation.

Justin hops up behind me, and, with no delay, binds my arms behind my back. He gags me with a red bandana and shoves me to the cold metal floorboard, all while Dawson looks on from outside the truck. "Good work," he tells Justin, chuckling. "Bind her up tight and good."

Justin dips his chin in a nod to Dawson, and then he crouches down behind me and secures the already tight knot at my wrists.

My hope of Justin becoming an ally plummets. Sealing my suspicion, my former coffee shop buddy makes it crystal clear he is *not* on my side when Dawson suddenly orders him to lower my jeans and panties, and he says flatly, "Okay. I'm on it."

What?

I try to scream, but I'm gagged. All that comes out is a strangled whimper. So, I cower, instead. But nothing stops Justin from completing the task he's been ordered to do.

He tugs my jeans and panties down to my knees, leaving me half-naked. "I hate you," I try to spit out from around my gag.

"Be quiet," he hisses. "You're only going to make it worse on yourself."

If I could spit at Justin, I would.

Fucker, I try to mutter, but it comes out as, "Och-ur,"

Appalled at this turn of events—*what are they planning on doing to me?*—I quickly scoot away, my ass moving swiftly along the cold metal truck floorboards. Grit and dirt scratch up the backs of my bare thighs and bare butt, but I couldn't care less. I just want to get away from the men. When I can't go any farther, I cower in the far corner.

The men watch me curiously, like I am a spectacle to be observed.

Let them watch, I think. I am too busy mentally preparing for the worst, as I suspect one—or both of them—will assault me next. I mean, come on. What's to stop them? I am semi-naked and vulnerable. And like in the alley, we are in an area devoid of people. Worse yet, Dawson makes no attempt to hide his prying eyes. He makes it all too clear he wants to see as much of me as he can. Justin, on the other hand, has the decency to look away.

Still, Dawson is frightening enough, and I can't help but

shake in fear and anger. Dawson, noticing my reaction, barks out an amused laugh. He points to a plastic bucket I hadn't noticed before. It's tucked away in the shadows of the corner opposite me.

When Dawson is done laughing, he says, "See that bucket over there? That's your toilet for the moment. Your pants are down so you can take a leak, you dumb bitch. You can quit acting like such a scared little animal."

Asshole. Though, admittedly, I feel minimally better that assault is not on his mind.

I breathe a little easier, until Dawson adds, "Then again, maybe I should have a taste of you while I have a chance."

Oh, God, no.

I close my eyes, and Justin murmurs, "Uh, I think we should probably get moving. There's no one around now, but this is New York. I'm sure someone will show up soon enough."

Thank you, Justin.

"Yeah," Dawson says resignedly, "I guess you're right."

When I dare to open my eyes, Dawson points at me menacingly. "Listen up. If you gotta go, now is the time. This will be your only chance for a long while. Better take advantage of my generosity, little girl, before I change my mind."

I cringe. *Generosity? Yeah right.* All I want is for my jeans and underwear to be back in place, covering my ass, like literally. However, I can't deny that my bladder does feel full.

I'm torn, though, on what to do. Do I nod my head *yes,* or shake my head *no.*

Indecisiveness renders me unmoving, and Dawson snaps, "Let me make it clear, Miss Brant. I don't plan on driving around with a bucket of piss in tow. So, again, you best take this opportunity." He flicks his hand, indicating the bucket. "Go ahead. Make it quick before we leave."

Guess I have no choice. And guess I'll have an audience.

Turning to Justin, Dawson says, "Go hold her up. She'll need help with her hands tied behind her back like that. When she's done, just make sure you empty that thing before we hit the road. I wasn't joking about the bucket of piss. I want that thing out of here."

Justin nods once. "Got it, sir," he says.

Dawson turns and disappears from sight. It's a small consolation, but I'll take it. If I have to pee in a bucket, I'd rather have an audience of just one.

That "just one" heads my way, grabbing up the bucket along his way. When Justin reaches where I'm now kneeling, he crouches down next to me.

"Um..." He looks away. "You need to spread some, Essa."

Oh my God. I open my knees wider and Justin wedges the bucket underneath me.

Neither of us makes eye contact, even as he holds my arm, helping me stay upright.

Ugh, I feel totally exposed, is all I can think. I know Justin can see everything, and I hate that humiliating fact.

"Do you have to go?" he quietly asks when nothing happens.

He glances at my face, and I nod, though I still can't meet his gaze. I have to go, now more than ever, but I'm so scared it's like some lever has been turned off.

I exhale, choking a little, and Justin lowers the gag from my mouth. "Here, maybe that will relax you a little."

"Thanks," I murmur, my voice rough.

Our eyes meet momentarily, but he quickly turns his head.

"I'll look the other way," he says. "That'll probably help, too, right?"

"Yes, probably," I whisper.

Justin twists his body away as much as he can while still steadying me. His averted eyes do help to relax me, though, as does not having the gag stuffed in my mouth. After a minute of intense concentration, a flow of urine starts.

Afterward, I exhale loudly and say, "Okay, I'm done."

Suddenly, I'm struck with the inanity of the whole situation. I feel almost giddy. *You're probably losing your mind from stress*, I reason.

Eyes still averted, Justin asks, "Do you need some toilet paper?"

In my new state of stressed-out-and-it's-better-to-joke-than-scream mentality, I say, "Yes, unless you prefer me to drip-dry."

Justin glances at me curiously, probably checking to see if I've lost my mind. After a beat, he says. "Okay, then, let me grab you some. Hold on a sec."

"Not like I'm going anywhere," I murmur.

Justin leans and balances his body so he can reach for the corner where the bucket was. He grabs at something, the toilet paper, I guess. For a minute, I can almost pretend he is the same guy I spent the past couple of weeks kidding around with in the coffee shop. But then, when he turns back to me, I realize I have no way to wipe myself.

Shit! I mentally kick myself for not keeping my stupid mouth shut. Justin is going to have to wipe me like I'm a toddler. I should have stuck with drip-drying. And I think I will...but before I open my mouth to protest, Justin places a big wad of toilet paper at my crotch.

I close my eyes. This is beyond humiliating, and I absolutely think I'm going to die, especially when he dabs lightly at my lady bits. He's actually trying to do a thorough job. *Kill me now.* I don't know whether to laugh or cry. Justin's careful touch isn't sexual in any way, not in the slightest. He's just helping me, I know, but nonetheless, I am horrified, horrified that another man, a guy who is not Farren, has his hand so close to my most private places.

Justin doesn't linger, though, and, at last, I open my eyes. "That good enough?" he asks, pulling the toilet paper away and sounding as embarrassed as I feel.

"Yes," I whisper.

He throws the wet paper in the bucket, and pulls up my panties and jeans. "There," he mutters with downcast eyes. As he stands and lifts the bucket, he adds, "I'm going to take this outside to empty it."

I don't respond, and I swear I hear him say under his breath, "I am so, so sorry, Essa."

I say, "What?" but he jumps down from the back of the truck too quickly to hear me or respond.

A minute or two later I hear voices outside, at the side of the truck. Justin is speaking with Dawson, but I can't discern what they're saying. Justin returns a few seconds later with the empty bucket. He tosses it in the far corner, away from where I'm seated. I watch as he rolls the garage-like rear door down tight, and from the outside, I hear Dawson locking it.

Great, we're locked in.

Resigned that we'll probably be on the road for a while, I lie down on my side. Curling up in a ball, I let go, emotion cut loose and tears falling freely. I cry tears of humiliation, tears of shame, tears of fear and not knowing what humiliating thing will happen next. I resign myself that this is the way Dawson plans to operate. His attacks on me will be psychological, like making me pee in a bucket with the help of a guy who spent the past couple of weeks making me think he was nice.

Ha, yeah right.

When Eric abducted Haven, he physically abused her from the start. I suspect the same thing will occur with me, and soon. Hell, Dawson already roughed me up and smacked me. Still, the not knowing when things might happen only serves to heighten the terror, make the whole ordeal more horrifying.

Justin sits across from me, in my line of sight. I try not to look at him, but when we start to move, I can't help but periodically peek over at him. Watching him is far more preferable to staring at the dingy truck interior and thinking about where I may end up.

As time passes, I note Justin seems rather nervous himself. He adjusts his glasses several times, swipes hair out of his eyes and off his forehead. He's definitely uneasy, giving the impression that he's in this mess far deeper than he ever intended.

Eventually, I grow tired. The low hum of the truck traveling on the open road—an interstate, maybe—lulls me into forgetting where I am. Instead, I'm reminded of far better times—my travels with Farren. I smile as memories wash over me, my recollections of how Farren and I fell in love as we traveled across the country.

I'm almost asleep, at peace, but then, out of the blue, Justin brings me back to the present when he blurts out, "I've seen girls pee before, you know. It's no big deal."

Oh, my God, shut up. Why is he dwelling on this?

It seems he wants to convey something when he continues.

"You should probably get over any embarrassment, Essa. Helping you like that isn't, like, a turn-on for me. Seeing your pus—, uh, I mean…whatever. The point is seeing you half-naked does nothing for me. I'm not interested in—"

"Just stop," I plead.

He glances over at me, but quickly looks away. "Never mind," he mutters. "I just thought you should know."

I stare at him harshly, and even though it might mean he'll gag me again, I scoff, "Seriously? What should I know that I don't? That you're a jerk who lied to me about who he was?"

"Think whatever you want," he retorts. "Your opinion means nothing to me."

For some reason, that comment hurts. "This can't be happening," I whisper. "I just want to go home."

"Hey, I'm sorry," Justin says.

"Shut up," I whisper, choking back a sob.

He continues, unfazed by my request. "Look, I am really sorry this is happening to you. If I could change things, I…" He falters, begins again, "I just never thought. I didn't know, Essa."

Hmm, is that regret? Maybe Justin could be an ally, after all.

In any case, he's my only option, so I press, "What are you saying, exactly?"

He leans his head back on the wall of the truck. "Never mind."

"No, Justin. What were you going to say?" I break into pleading mode, begging him, "Please, let me go. Can you do that?" I rise to my knees, my bound arms unbalancing me. I rock back on my heels—that's better. "Please, Justin, please. You sound like you regret helping Dawson. This is how you can make things better. At the next stop, help me get away. If you can just divert Dawson's attention—"

"There won't be any stops, Essa," Justin interrupts, sighing. "So, I couldn't help you even if I wanted to."

"But, you want to, don't you?"

"Just stop asking for something that isn't going to happen, okay?"

I collapse, the back of my head hitting the wall of the truck. "Ouch."

Justin ignores me, and I ask, "Where are we going, anyway?"

He shrugs. "Upstate New York, I think, someplace in the Adirondacks. I'm not sure, but I overheard Dawson on the phone, mentioning something about an abandoned ski resort."

Oh hell, no. Nobody will ever find me at some abandoned, forlorn location. Maybe not even Farren.

In a last ditch attempt, I appeal to Justin once more. "If you help get me away from Dawson, I won't tell anyone you were involved."

"What about your boyfriend?"

How in the hell does Justin know about him? I never once mentioned Farren to him. Dawson must have told him.

"I won't say a word to Farren," I fib. Because, come on, I don't keep anything from him, just like he tells me everything.

Justin waves his hand around aimlessly, and says, "It doesn't matter. I can't help you, anyway."

"Why the hell not? You do know Dawson is an awful person, right? He's a danger to both of us, Justin. Do you really think he's just going to let you walk away from this? He won't. You're a witness to everything he's done. He'll—"

"Enough!" he snaps. "I know all that, okay? That's why I can't help you. He'll kill me if I do. You know that's true."

He has a point. But I sense remorse in his helplessness. Justin isn't completely averse to helping me. If we had a good enough plan, then maybe…

Sighing, I ask, "How'd you ever get involved in this, anyway?"

He eyes me apologetically. "I hate to admit it, but I signed on for the cash. I need the money to finish school."

"Offering me up for slaughter for money," I sourly state. "That's really nice."

Justin glares at me, his brown eyes snapping behind his lenses. "It's not anything like that. I had no idea things would go this far. Dawson said he just needed to talk to you. He said you were afraid of him, but that there was no good reason for you to feel that way. I never dreamt he'd kidnap you, or take you out of the city." Slamming the back of his head against the inside wall of the truck, he grinds out, "Fuck, this is such a mess."

"Justin…"

Closing his eyes, he whispers, "My life is a mess, Essa. My parents quit talking to me months ago. That's why I need the money. They cut me off after…"

He trails off, and I quietly ask, "Why did your parents quit talking to you? What made them cut you off like that?"

Justin barks out a humorless laugh. "Let's just say they don't exactly approve of my, uh, lifestyle choices."

And I know then what he's trying to say. His earlier remark about not being interested in seeing me half-naked suddenly makes sense, as does how he went on and on about how I shouldn't let it bother me so much that he had to help me go to the bathroom in the bucket.

"Your parents cut you off because you're gay?" I say, incredulous and aghast that people can still be so closed-minded.

"Yep," Justin says, his gaze falling on me, assessing me for *my* reaction.

"I have no problem with that," I tell him, in case he thinks for some crazy reason I would feel otherwise.

"Okay, good." He sighs.

He looks so hurt, it's clear his parents have really done a number on him. "I'm sorry," I say.

He shrugs. "Hey, what can you do?"

I have no answer, so we both fall silent. It's like that for a while, until I say, "This feels so weird." I nod to the space between us. "I mean, here we are sharing...*a lot*...and look at the circumstances."

"Right," he replies, nodding and smiling. "It is kind of weird."

I smile over at him, but then, realizing the direness of my circumstances, I swallow the lump that forms in my throat.

Justin sighs, his gaze softening. "Listen, Essa, I'll help you, okay?"

"Yeah, right." A single sob escapes me. "Why bother?"

"I'm serious," he says, lowering his voice to a whisper. "I promise you that I don't want to see you get hurt. I hated watching Dawson hit you. He's seriously fucked-up."

"No shit," I interject.

He clears his throat. "I want to help you, and I'm going to help you, but first, Essa, you have to realize I'll need to act like you are nothing to me when"—he jerks his head to the cabin of the truck—"he's around."

"Okay," I agree. "That makes sense."

We travel, mostly in silence, for a few more hours. And then, with a lurch, the truck turns off the highway and, shortly after that, onto a bumpy, rutted road.

Justin sighs. "I'm going to have to put the gag back in. We've been traveling for a while now. We'll be stopping soon."

"Yeah,"—I nod—"okay."

When I'm once again silenced, my eyes meet Justin's apologetic gaze. He says nothing, but his sad smile and his soulful browns behind the bookworm glasses convey that we are in this together now.

And that is infinitely better than being in it alone.

CHAPTER FIVE

Farren

OUTSIDE the coffee shop, around the corner, there's a narrow, darkened alley. The sun is setting, bathing the loading docks and wooden pallets strewn about in an eerie yellow glow.

"Here goes nothing," I mutter to myself before starting down the narrow passageway.

It becomes clear rather quickly that this alley is used for early morning deliveries, not for parking. Nevertheless, in typical big city park-wherever-you-can mentality, a few vehicles are wedged in here and there among the overflowing dumpsters and awkwardly stacked towers of cardboard delivery boxes.

The surrounding tall buildings, most made of brick, are dingy and dirty, dimming the alley further. I imagine how dark the alley must have been earlier, with the brick structures obscuring the afternoon sun.

Final conclusion: this is just the sort of abduction point

Dawson would choose.

Glancing about, however, I find nothing blatantly amiss. Well, that's the case until a small piece of metal, glinting in the dying light of the sinking sun, catches my eye.

I crouch down to take a better look and recognize the shiny object immediately.

"This is Essa's cell phone charm," I muse as I push the gravel away from the pink heart, the charm Haven gave Essa recently.

The trinket is in pristine condition, meaning it's only been here in the dirt and gravel for a short while. "Essa was definitely in this alley earlier today," I whisper to myself.

This news simultaneously disturbs and elates me. I am disturbed because without a doubt Essa was abducted here, probably in this very same spot. The elation I feel stems from the fact my girlfriend was smart enough to leave me a clue. *Good job, Essa.*

Still crouched, but shifting to get more comfortable, I examine the surrounding area, searching for more clues. My trained eyes know exactly what to look for, and I soon conclude, based on shoe impressions in the gravel, that there were three people gathered in this small space.

Three, not two. Interesting.

Dawson had a helper, just as I suspected. It had to be the guy I learned of today—Justin.

I find a few partial prints among the shoe impressions, but many are fully intact, which will help in identifying who is who. I conclude from simple observation that two of the sets were made by men, lending further credence to my Justin-was-Dawson's-helper theory. The third set of shoe impressions are small, surely made by Essa.

"Shit, baby, what happened here?" I ask the dead air as I rub my temple. I half expect Essa to appear and answer, but that, of course, doesn't happen.

The stress is wearing on me, clearly. But back to analyzing the scene I am somewhat relieved to find there's no evidence indicating any sort of a major struggle. Of course, that also means one of the men, if not both, had a weapon. Otherwise, Essa would have tried to run. She had to have known she'd already made one huge mistake by trusting the guy from the coffee shop; she wouldn't make a second error.

Sighing, I get to work on gathering more evidence. I take measurements and samples of the dirt and gravel left in the shoeprints. I also analyze the single set of tire tracks made by the getaway vehicle. I need to know what kind of car was used to whisk Essa away so I can match it up with any traffic cam data I'm able to access. Based on the width of the tire impressions, it appears the getaway car was a small, compact vehicle. Still, I can't be sure of a make or model until I enter the data into a program I have on a computer back at the apartment. After I run the measurements the possibilities will be narrowed to only a few, same with the shoeprints.

Dawson is in my database back in my "war room," as I like to call it. I should be able to identify him immediately. The second set of impressions could pose a problem, though. I have no way of linking them with Justin, as I doubt he's in any criminal databases.

Rocking back on my heels, I hate that what I feared all along has occurred. Dawson employed someone around Essa's age to trick her, and it worked like a charm. Ironic that the naivety I found so attractive in Essa, especially at the beginning of our relationship, has been exploited by someone with bad intentions.

I can't help but wonder what other ways Essa will be exploited before this is all over.

"Fuck," I mutter, No, I can't even go there.

Shaking my head, dispelling my lurid thoughts, I take out my cell and call Rick. No need for him to remain out west when Dawson is clearly on this side of the country.

Answering immediately, Rick says, "What's up, Farren?"

He sounds like he's in a good mood, and why wouldn't he be. He and Vincent sit around and shoot the breeze when things are quiet, and I know things have been damn near silent out there since all the shit is going down here.

I blow out a breath, and tell him, "We have a problem here in New York."

"What kind of problem?"

"The kind I can't talk about on the phone." The line is supposed to be secure, but I can't take any chances. "I'll tell you more when I see you."

"See me?" Rick sounds confused, as the plan up till now has been for him to remain in New Mexico until Dawson was spotted.

"Yeah," I sigh. "I need for you to fly out to New York City as soon as possible."

Without skipping a beat, Rick wants to know, "Is Haven okay?"

Despite what's going down, I have to chuckle. Rick likes my sister, a lot. That's cool with me, though, as I've known the guy for over a decade. Hell, he's had my back in hundreds of life and death situations. Bottom line, Rick is one of the good guys out there, and Haven would be forever safe if she ended up with him.

Can't ask for more than that, especially with all the creeps out there in the world. Protecting Haven seems more important than ever with Essa gone.

Shuddering, I finally reply to Rick's question. "Yes," I say, "Haven is fine."

Rick sounds relieved, I hear him swallowing hard on the other end. "Good," he says, "that's good."

Quietly, I add, "There's another problem, though. A big one and it involves Essa."

"Shit," Rick curses under his breath. He knows what's up. "Dawson?" he questions.

I stare down at the shoe tracks, the largest of the three. "Yeah, I think so."

"Hold it together, Shaw," Rick says. He knows I love Essa in a way I never knew was possible. I can handle a million situations with no emotion, but *this* is not one of them.

When I don't respond, seeing as I'm just trying to keep my breathing even, Rick immediately says, "Hey, listen. I'll be on a plane within the hour."

CHAPTER SIX

Essa

THE rutted road leading to the abandoned ski resort seems never-ending. The truck slows in spots, sometimes unbearably so, but we keep on moving. I am jostled about, as there are many twists and turns. We are definitely ascending, heading up into the mountains.

My ears pop with the rising elevation, while Justin remains quiet. He's been that way for a while. I remain in forced silence, the gag returned to my mouth. We hit an especially rough patch of road, and I am thrown forward. My bound arms are not much use in balancing me, so, as we come to a rolling stop, I am on my side, facing the side of the truck. I have no way to right myself and assume Justin has fallen asleep. Otherwise, he would help me sit up.

Suddenly, with the truck apparently parked, the back door rolls up, slowly and tortuously. I cringe, knowing this means more interaction with Dawson. Holding my breath, I count to ten, then slowly exhale. *Gotta stay calm, gotta stay focused.*

Count to ten again, exhale.

Even with the back door all the way up, no light filters in. It's the middle of the night, yes, but I still expected some illumination. We must be in an extremely remote location. Apart from the utter darkness, everything is quiet as can be.

The silence is almost peaceful, until Dawson barks out, "Wake the hell up, you two!"

I hear Justin come to life, springing into action. "Sorry, sir," he says in a rush, "I wasn't sleeping. Not fully, anyway. I only closed my eyes for a minute, I swear."

Dawson harrumphs. "You're supposed to be watching Miss Brant, not napping. You're paid to keep your eyes on her, not closed."

"Yes, sir, I know, sir."

I hear movement behind me, and Dawson yells, "Well, why are you still sitting there adjusting your fucking glasses? Wake the bitch up."

"Okay, okay."

Justin shuffles around some more, and then snaps at me, "Get up, Essa."

His sneakered foot nudges at my back, and when I don't move, he yells, "Get the hell up, fucking whore."

I know Justin is playing a role, talking tough to me in order to fool Dawson, just like we agreed. Still, it stings to hear such harsh words.

"I can't," I grumble from around the gag.

It's true. Without the use of my hands, all I can do is roll to my back. I do exactly that, and Justin grabs me by my shoulders and hauls me to my feet, turning me to face Dawson in the process.

As usual, the sight of the foul man makes my blood run cold.

Dawson seems to be enjoying my reactions, especially me cowering in fear. He smiles coldly and says, "You don't like me very much, Miss Brant, do you?"

Since a positive response, even a simple nod, would please him, I remain motionless.

"Ah, not to worry," he continues, unaffected. "I have a feeling we'll become quite close very soon."

I'm done showing restraint with this asshole. I'm doomed anyway, so I narrow my eyes at him, showing him my disgust.

Dawson chuckles. "Oh, you think you're some kind of tough girl now? Hanging out with Shaw seems to have given you false confidence." Turning away from me, he says to Justin, "Bring her to me."

"No," I try to yell, but all that comes out with the gag in my mouth is a muffled "*nnn*" sound.

Justin hauls me over to Dawson, and I am made to kneel, placing me face-to-face with the man I despise. He steps closer to the edge of the truck, and I have no choice but to peer into the meanest eyes I've ever seen. In the darkness, it's as if I'm staring into coal black pits of Hell. His hatred for me is palpable, singeing the air. I fear the man might actually climb up into the truck, right now, and do God knows what to me.

In the interest of remaining unharmed, I avert my gaze, and Dawson remarks, "Wise move."

To Justin, he says, "Take the gag out so she can speak."

Justin complies, but words elude me. My mouth is dry and parched, and my throat is sore. I swallow a couple of times, big gasps for air, and Dawson watches me like I am his pet. I suppose, in a way, I am, at least until I'm rescued.

"Aah, we'll get you some water," he says softly, his leathery hand reaching out to touch my face.

Disgusting, I think, and instinct takes over. I jerk back, crying out a repulsed, "No!"

Anger flashes in Dawson's beady eyes, and he raises his hand. I flinch, expected to be hit, like earlier. But no strike comes. Instead, Dawson touches my face gently with his cool, dry fingers. In a way, his soft ministrations are far worse than being struck.

Fingers that feel like dried paper caress my face in a falsely loving manner. Dawson coos, "So soft, so delicate..." He sucks in a breath, his tongue coming out like a reptile. "I see why Shaw finds you so irresistible."

Everything about this man disgusts me, but it repulses me further to think Dawson really believes he knows what Farren feels when he touches me. How dare this man presume to know what true love is all about?

I want to speak out, but I don't dare say a single word. Doing so could push Dawson too far, as I am well aware his gentle caresses are nothing more than a farce.

"So tense," he continues, his fingers rubbing my clenched jaw. "Loosen up, Essa. What I have to share with you might open your eyes. In fact, for your sake, it better."

Curious, I ask, "What's that supposed to mean?"

"In due time, my dear, in due time you'll find out everything, all the truths that have been kept from you. But for now, let's just say your dear Farren Shaw is not who you think he is."

"Yeah, right," I mumble, and that causes Dawson to jerk his hand from my face.

"He's no knight in shining armor," he snaps.

"I never said he was," I counter. "But I do know Farren is a good and loving man. He's decent…not like you. And nothing you have to say will ever change my mind about him."

Justin nudges me in my back, like he's trying to tell me now might be a good time to zip it. But I can't hold my tongue; I can't let this vile man continue to think he can somehow turn me against Farren. How ludicrous.

"I love Farren," I go on, feeling more and more emboldened. "And I know he's done some bad things. But every action he takes is for a greater good of some kind, whether to save a life—"

Dawson cuts me off with a deep, rumbling laugh. "Oh, this is too good. The big, bad wolf has the little girl so blinded by love she can't even see the truth."

"Farren's not a wolf," I protest. "*You're* the wolf."

"Is that supposed to be an insult?" Dawson smirks. "Farren is the same as I. We are both wolves, Miss Brant. Only difference is I don't pretend to be something I am not."

"It's not the only difference," I mutter.

That earns me a sharp jab in the back from Justin. "Shut the hell up," he hisses.

When I see the look on Dawson's face, I know Justin is right. It's time to shut up.

"Take her inside," Dawson snaps to Justin.

"Yes, sir," Justin flatly replies. "On it now, sir."

Dawson steps away. He doesn't leave, though. He stands at the side of the truck, watching as Justin helps me down to the ground. I am unsteady from sitting so long and I waver left and right.

Dawson, stepping uncomfortably close to me, steadies me with a firm hand to my elbow, and I almost scream, "Get your hands off me."

Of course, I do nothing of the kind.

"You best come to see things my way," Dawson whispers to me, leaning in even closer. "Otherwise, things can get very unpleasant for you, very quickly."

He stomps away, leaving me with Justin.

Right then, the wind picks up and I shiver. Not from the cold nighttime mountain air, but from Dawson's icy words, still hanging in the air.

CHAPTER SEVEN

Farren

RICK arrives at my New York apartment in the middle of the night. The late hour doesn't matter much, seeing as I've been up for hours, completely unable to sleep. My concern for Essa seems to have increased exponentially with each passing minute. I've found relief only in working in the war room. I feel as if I have to stay busy in order to stay sane.

This is so unlike me, though, this edgy man I am becoming. But it is what it is. How Essa has woven her way into my heart to this extent defies logic. But she has. My old self would've remained impassive, guided by logic. These days, though, when it comes to Essa it's my heart that rules. And let's just say the heart speaks an entirely different language than the brain.

When I feel as if I need a break from the madness, I step out into the hallway. On my third such trip, I hear knocking at the front door. At this late hour it can only be Rick.

I pass Haven in the living room, noticing she's fallen asleep on the sofa, one hand under a pillow. In her other hand, she clutches a heart-shaped cell phone charm, the red one that matches Essa's pink charm. I look away.

After I let Rick in to the apartment I fill him in on all that has happened, relaying everything I couldn't say on the phone. We then head to the war room, where Rick makes a quick phone call to Vincent, our FBI contact, in order to touch base.

"He knows there's trouble," Rick says to me before Vincent picks up. "Give me a few minutes to get him up to speed."

I nod. "Yeah, sure, take your time. Vincent on the team is a welcome addition."

When Rick disconnects, a few minutes later, he tells me, "Vincent flew to DC after I talked to you yesterday. And he just now confirmed he's more than willing to help with the case from headquarters."

Essa's disappearance is now a "case." *Great*, I think, saddened that things have come to this. It's so wrong, so off. Essa should be here at the apartment, not out there, in danger.

Raking my hand through my hair, I say, "Yeah, okay. Vincent on the case can only help."

It will, too, in a number of ways. Vincent has access to some FBI databases even I can't tap into. His help could prove invaluable in finding Essa. Still, even with this good piece of news, I remain wrecked. I must look pretty bad, too, since Rick puts a hand on my shoulder and says in a low tone, "You holding up okay, man?"

He's never seen me rattled, not like this. And we've been through hundreds of hostile situations, situations beyond your worst imaginings. But this, this thing with Essa, it has me twisted up inside like nothing else, ever.

"Yeah,"—I nod reassuringly—"I'm good."

Rick eyes me skeptically. "You sure, 'cause you look like hell, Shaw."

"Yeah, I'm sure. It's just that…" I trail off, unable to articulate my deepest fear that Essa might not make it back alive.

Swiftly, and to change the subject, I grab up one of Rick's bags that he lugged in to the war room. Swinging the door open, I motion for Rick to follow. "Come on, I'll show you your room. We'll drop these bags off, and then we can get to work."

Rick nods as he picks up his other bag. He knows I need a distraction. "Sure," he says, "sounds good."

Halfway down the hall, I nod to a bedroom with an open door. "You can sleep in here." When he glances over to a bedroom with a closed door, I tell him, "That's Haven's room, but she's not in there. She fell asleep on the sofa."

"How's she holding up with Essa gone?" Rick wants to know.

I shake my head. "Not good."

Rick leans against the doorframe of his designated room and observes me. He knows when my mind is on family.

"How about in other ways?" he asks.

"What do you mean?"

Rick lets out a long sigh. "Well, you know I talk to Haven all the time"—I nod—"and she's always upbeat, telling me how great the acting workshops are, how much she likes the city, shit like that. But when I ask her how she's doing, like, *really* doing, she brushes me off. She's a fucking pro at hiding her feelings, Shaw. You giving her lessons?"

I laugh. "Like she'd listen to me."

"Good point."

"Hey," I continue, "Haven does keep her emotions bottled up.

You're right about that. It's a Shaw family trait, yeah, but don't give up on her."

"Never," Rick assures me. "You know how I feel about your sister."

"Yeah, I know," I quietly reply.

After a beat, I add, "If you want to look in on Haven before we get back to work, that's cool with me. Like I said, she's out in the living room."

Rick appears relieved, like he wanted to ask, but just didn't know if it was appropriate under the circumstances.

"Thanks," he replies. "I don't want to wake her , but I'd like to see her for a minute."

Rick wants to look in on Haven even if she is fast asleep because he cares. Same as I'd give anything right now to be able to look in on Essa.

Turning to head down the hall, I say over my shoulder, "Take your time, man. I'll be in the war room."

A few minutes later Rick rejoins me in the war room and we get straight to work. First up is further analysis of the samples I gathered from the scene of Essa's abduction. Based on the tire track info I input into my special program, I come up with the getaway car make and model.

"An older model Toyota Corolla," I say, reading the info scrolling on the screen.

"You got an image?" Rick asks from a chair across from me.

"Sure do." A photo emerges from the printer. "I got this from the traffic cam outside the coffee shop."

Rick picks up the photo and examines it carefully. "This must have been taken when they were leaving," he says. "It's a little blurry, but you can make out three individuals in the car, two in the front and one in the back."

He hands me the photo. It's grainy, like he said, but I have no doubt the female in the back is Essa.

"We have to find that car," Rick says.

"Yeah, but I'm sure they've swapped out to something else by now. We need to find out what they switched over to."

"Let me secure a line with Vincent," Rick says. "See what he came up with."

Once we're online with Vincent, he sends us what he's procured thus far, mostly more traffic cam footage from around the city. After swiping through a number of images popping up on the computer screen, I finally locate the Corolla.

"They headed north through Manhattan," I observe.

Rick comes around to my side of the table and leans in as I go through shots showing the progression of the car. "Looks like they drove Essa up to Harlem," he muses.

I freeze-frame on a shot of the Corolla pulling in to a parking space near Grant's Tomb. "That's where they stopped."

We print out several still photos from the area as Vincent feeds them to us.

"After the Toyota was ditched..." I flip through the printed images. "...it looks like Essa was led to a box truck by two men."

"Dawson, we're definitely dealing with Dawson," Rick adds when the printer spits out a close-up shot of Essa and her captors.

"As if there was any doubt," I reply as he hands me the photo.

The image shows Essa, flanked by Dawson and a young man with reddish hair and glasses. I finally get a good look at Justin, and I see right away how he got the drop on Essa. He's completely innocuous, or so he appears. God, I hope he really is an innocuous individual. I pray he's too much of a good guy to take part in Dawson's surely horrific plans for Essa.

But all I have is hope and prayers, and, sadly, most of the time that is not enough. *God, I need some sleep.*

Rick catches me rubbing my eyes and yawning, and says, "You should get some sleep, Farren. I slept on the flight. I can work on this stuff for a while longer if you want to lie down for a few."

"No, I should stay up."

"Hey," Rick counters, "you're of no use to anyone if you're exhausted. Go rest. I'll wake you up if I come across anything ground-breaking."

"Yeah, okay." I stand, relenting. "Don't let me sleep more than a few hours, though, okay?"

"You got it," Rick says.

EXHAUSTED as I am, sleep finds me quickly. And my dreams are filled with Essa, images of her body beneath my hands, recalls of how soft her skin feels, especially when her arms and legs are wrapped around me.

In my dream I am with her, connected to her, body and soul. My body rocks with hers, gently, so gently. But despite me going easy on her, she comes undone. Fuck, I am buried so deeply inside her I can feel her milking every inch of my shaft. I come right after her, and I feel so wanted, so accepted. Essalin accepts all of me, good and bad. At least, in my dreams she does.

Her hand is on my cheek. "Not just in your dreams," she tells me with a smile. "I accept you, Farren, in every way. And that means I accept *everything* you've ever done."

Oh, how I wish this was not a dream.

"You don't know everything, Essa," I reply. "You don't know anything about the things I've done. And you certainly have no clue of the things I still do. If you only knew what I did just last week—"

"Stop, Farren." Her hand covers my mouth, and she smiles as she circles her hips, her body beneath me. "I don't care," she goes on. "Love is about acceptance, and I love you." Another circle of her hips, and she urges, "Move with me, Farren. Make love to me."

Just as I begin to move, flooded with feelings of urgency and relief, a knock at my bedroom door jars me awake.

"Shit." Rolling to my back, I call out, "Hold up a sec." I give myself a minute to calm down, as I'm aroused from my dream.

When my dick goes down, I call out, "Come in."

Rick opens the door just an inch. "We got something on Essa," he says.

I sit up abruptly. "What is it?"

"Not sure, maybe a possible location."

I am standing in an instant, my feet having hit the floor in two seconds flat.

CHAPTER EIGHT

Essa

THE abandoned ski resort in the Adirondacks is kind of creepy. Desolate and lonely, the air feels cool and thin. Mountains appear as dark shadows in the background as Justin leads me along a narrow and overgrown path. The surrounding forest is thick with summer foliage, dense and dark. A large lake shimmers to the left as we close in on a ramshackle ski chalet, my new prison.

My arms are still bound behind my back, having been tied that way for hours now, and I can honestly say I hurt all over. My cheek throbs from where Dawson hit me, and my bit lip is scabbed over. Additionally, I am mentally weary and physically exhausted.

"Can we slow down a little?" I ask when I almost trip over an exposed tree root.

"No." Justin steadies me and urges me forward. "We can't

stop, Essa. Dawson is waiting for us up at the chalet." He jerks his chin to a shadowy A-frame building several yards away. "He can see us, I'm sure. Slowing down will look suspicious."

"Yeah," I concede. "You have a point."

I don't want to jeopardize our newly forged alliance in any way, so I try harder to keep up with Justin's long strides. When we near the chalet, a cedar structure a stone's throw from the dilapidated main resort, Dawson steps out into the open doorway, his trim figure blocking the entrance. He crosses his arms and leans up against the frame. Standing there, completely still, he watches our slow but steady approach with a bemused grin.

I don't care to know what has him smiling this time, so I focus on the chalet. There are a few lights on inside the structure, casting a sickly yellow glow, and backlighting Dawson in the doorway like a looming monster. Sneaky bastard, he must have set up a makeshift generator to provide power for our stay. A slippery man such as he would know exactly how to rig this old dump to make it somewhat inhabitable.

"How long do you think we'll stay here?" I whisper to Justin.

"I don't know," he replies softly. "But I'm sure when Dawson is done here, when he takes you somewhere else, I'll be sent on my way."

"If you're lucky," I mutter.

"I know, right." Justin laughs hollowly. "I doubt he'll let me off the hook so easily."

He knows as well as I do that Dawson is using him, and when this gig is up it is highly doubtful Justin will be permitted to just walk away.

I open my mouth to say something, but then I notice Dawson cocking his head, observing Justin and me curiously.

Does he know Justin has turned? That he's helping me now? We can't have that, not this early in the game, so to sidetrack the old fool, I purposely trip.

When Justin attempts to keep me from falling, I hiss under my breath, "Don't be so gentle. Dawson is watching us. I tripped on purpose, make it look good."

Justin responds in kind by yanking me up and pushing me forward.

"Pick up the pace," he barks out, loudly enough for Dawson to hear. "Quit trying to stall."

Justin's fake bad treatment of me seems to appease Dawson.

Smiling, he yells out, "Good work, Justin. You're learning. Keep her moving."

We close in on the chalet, stopping when we are a few feet from the doorway.

Dawson, focusing solely on me, says, a little too gleefully, "There's someone here who can't wait to meet you, Essa, our lovely, new fresh meat."

I don't know who is here to meet me—the fresh meat, how lovely—but I suspect the shadow of a rather large man hovering behind Dawson is the person he is referring to.

I sarcastically utter, "Oh, great," but all I really want to do right now is twist from Justin's grasp and run the hell away. I wouldn't get too far, though, not with three men on my tail.

Dawson steps aside and, like some demented proprietor of this dark place, says, "Welcome, Miss Brant. We're going to make sure you thoroughly enjoy your stay."

He cackles, amused with his obnoxious self, and I promptly ignore him. Justin does the same as he leads me in to what was once the lobby of the chalet. You can tell it was nice at one time, but not anymore.

What a wreck. I take in the plaster peeling from the walls and the ceiling, many of the curled bits littering the floor. Old, faded brochures lie strewn about, tipped from a mangled rack. The whole side of a dark wood check-in counter is caved in, and the smell of the lobby is putrid, damp and musty. Bottom line, the place is frightful, and as if confirming that observation, a plump rat promptly scurries by.

Ugh.

I squeeze in close to Justin, but wisely staying in character, he shoves me away. And it's when I am righting myself that I notice the man Dawson made reference to, the one who couldn't wait to meet me, or rather the man who couldn't wait to meet what I represent—fresh meat. The hulking figure I saw only as a shadow steps forward and takes his place next to Dawson.

His dull, empty eyes scan me from head to toe, and then he growls out, "Nice one, boss." Rubbing a meaty paw over his bald head, he leers. "She's very pretty. When do I get some alone-time with this one?"

I shudder. I despise this man—a guard, based on his bulk—already. His expression conveys to me just how much he'd like to "get me alone." It is crystal clear that any time spent with this guy would involve him hurting me, badly.

I can't help but cower back into Justin, but, again, he nudges me away. *Smart move.* Too bad I'm having trouble remaining as calm as him.

The big guard takes a menacing step toward me, but Dawson grabs his thick arm. Tsking, he says, "Not just yet, Pierson. Not unless she deserves it."

Dawson then spins to me, like a villain in a bad movie. Too

bad this is real. "Miss Brant," he says. "Let me warn you that should you try to escape I will not hesitate to give Pierson here a minimum of thirty minutes alone with you. And let me tell you, little one, the last few women who spent even *ten* minutes alone with Pierson were, unfortunately"—he throws back his head and laughs—"never quite the same."

Pierson spits out a chortle of his own, joining in with Dawson's amusement at the proposition of harm being done to me, irreparable harm.

God, I have to get out of here.

When the two are done having their fun, Dawson pins me with his shark-like stare. "So, no escape attempts, right?"

"Right," I rasp. I clear my throat, which is constricted from fear. "No escape attempts, I promise." *Lie.*

I feel Justin's hand on my back start to shake, and I suspect his commitment to help me may be waning. Not that escape will be easy anyway. Besides the frightening Pierson we now have to contend with, I know for a fact Dawson won't let his guard down for even one second.

Even if a chance to run does arise, how will I ever get out?

From what I can observe as I glance left and right, every window and every door in the chalet is boarded up securely. The front door we came through appears to be the only way out.

I am so screwed, and I feel torn between giving up and falling apart, and sticking with the program.

I decide to stick with the program, which means never giving up. And if there is one hope that still holds me together it's that Farren will find me.

I just pray he finds me quickly.

CHAPTER NINE

Farren

THERMAL heat imaging of abandoned locations in upstate New York tips us off as to where Essa has mostly likely been taken.

After following a trail of traffic cam footage, showing the box truck Essa was placed in heading out of the city and northbound through the state, Rick sent Vincent a list of potential hideouts in the upstate New York area.

Sophisticated FBI software got a hit! Heat was detected—in the form of people, not animals—at a location in the Adirondacks, a ski resort that's been closed for years.

"Four people are in a chalet up there," Vincent told us. "But we can't be sure of their gender."

"Doesn't matter," I replied. "I know Essa is one of the four. Dawson and Justin are two of the others." I had no clue on the identity of the fourth person, and I didn't like that one bit.

But there's no more time to worry about it. We leave for upstate New York as soon as possible.

In the war room Rick and I are prepping to go. We are in the midst of deciding which guns—and how much firepower in general—to take with us.

Pausing with my favorite .45 in hand, I say, "You know we can't go in there with guns blazing. Dawson will kill Essa if he thinks I have him dead to rights."

Rick is mounting a scope on a rifle, and he stops and looks over at me. "I know," he says, sighing. "I've actually been thinking the exact same thing." Placing the rifle on the table, he crosses his arms across his chest. "Even if we get a jump on Dawson, we still don't know who this other guy is…and that could pose a problem,"

"No doubt," I say, setting the .45 down. Raking a hand through my hair, I add, "I'm sure the other guy is a guard."

"Yeah, most likely"

"Well, at least we're relatively certain Justin won't be a problem," I state encouragingly.

"That's true."

And it is. We ID'd Justin. He really is a student, lives in Jersey, and his full name is Justin Bauer.

"Still," I say, "depending on who the guard is, anything can happen."

"Exactly," Rick replies.

"I don't like that kind of uncertainty," I muse as I grab a box of ammo.

A soft knock on the closed war room door places our conversation on hold. "Hey, it's me," Haven calls out from the hallway. "Is it okay if I come in?"

Rick glances at me questioningly, and I nod. "Sure, let her in."

I can't help but notice Rick smiling surreptitiously as he heads to the door. When he opens it, Haven's eyes widen. "Rick!" she exclaims, throwing her arms around his large body as best as she can. "I can't believe you're really here in New York."

We've been locked up in the war room for hours, apart from my short sleep break. Haven had no way of knowing Rick was here, but she sure as hell knows now.

"I'm really here," he assures her with an adoring squeeze.

He then closes his eyes and holds on to my sister for a while longer. There's such genuine affection in their reunion that I feel I should turn away. But before I can move, they break apart, stepping away from each other like they're suddenly aware of my presence.

"Sorry," Rick murmurs.

Haven glances at me uneasily.

I roll my eyes. "No need to act all shy around me," I remark. "I know you two are, shall we say, more than friends."

Rick coughs, and I chuckle. Haven mutters under her breath, "Jeez, Farren, enough already."

And then she eyes Rick with a sly smile. I know it then, my best friend and my sister love each other. It's sweet and endearing, especially in these early stages. Maybe they haven't even admitted it to themselves, but it's clear they have fallen head over heels. I'm sure Essa and I appear the same to the rest of the world.

My smile fades at the thought of Essa and the danger she is in. I hastily get back to the business at hand.

"So, Haven," I begin, turning to my sister. "Rick and I are leaving the apartment in less than an hour. We should go over some things before we go."

"Wait," she says. "Where are you going?"

"Upstate."

With a sweeping glance around the room at all the firepower on display, she says. "I'm guessing you found Essa?"

"Yes," I reply as I set aside another box of ammo to take. Seems like there may never be enough bullets to relieve the tension I feel.

"Dawson has her, doesn't he?" Haven asks.

"Yes," I reply. "It's definitely Dawson who has her."

Looking from me to Rick, and then back to me, Haven states, "I want to help, Farren. Essa helped out when you were looking for me. It's my turn to return the favor, if you can even call it that. Anyway, just tell me what to do, and I'll do it. I can even go with you if you want."

No way. Though I find it endearing that my sister, after all she's been through, is still willing and ready to help her friend. Unfortunately, this situation is far too dangerous to involve Haven in any meaningful way.

I explain this to Haven, in those exact words, and then add, "I need you to stay put, okay?"

"Are you saying you want me to, like, stick around the apartment the whole time?" She makes a distasteful face. "You want me to skip my acting workshops and just stay inside?"

"Yes," I reply. "And I'm sorry, Hav. I know it'll be boring as hell, but staying inside the apartment is the only safe option. In fact, apart from surveillance already in place, I have someone coming to guard you while we're gone."

Rick nods in agreement. "Yeah, babe, stay inside the building. The guard can get you whatever you need."

"Okay," Haven replies, relenting. "I'll stay here, but only if you promise to keep me updated."

"Of course," I assure her.

Rick breathes out a sigh of relief that Haven is not putting up a fight, or insisting on accompanying us. Haven, seeing his expression, smiles over at him.

Annnd, there's my cue.

Now would be a good time to let them talk, since we only have a short while before we take off.

"I'm going to go pack some clothes," I say, waving my hand toward the door. "Take some time, catch up."

My sister says, "Thanks, Farren," while Rick gives me an appreciative upward nod.

Once in the hall, I close the door behind me. And then I need a moment to decompress, before things get crazy. Feeling for the wall behind me, I lean back and grind out a frustrated, "Fuck."

The summer wasn't supposed to go down like this. I was supposed to keep Essa safe while Rick and Vincent searched for Dawson. But the bastard outsmarted us. No one expected him to sneak in to New York and snatch Essa out from under my nose.

If only I hadn't been out of the country, things may have gone down differently.

And that reminds me of another pressing problem. How much longer do I keep Essa in the dark over what I do for the agency?

I know she deserves the truth. And if we're ever to move beyond mere boyfriend and girlfriend status, Essa needs to know, she deserves to know what she's getting into with me. And that means all the facts of my *whole* life, not just parts of it. Armed with full disclosure, she can make a decision on whether she wants to stay with me…or leave.

Though the thought of her leaving makes my throat constrict. "Shit."

A clock chimes somewhere in my apartment, reminding me that time is running out. Not just in regards to rescuing Essa, but quite possibly on my time with her in general.

CHAPTER TEN

Essa

I AM given a tiny room in which to stay. I term it *my ski chalet prison*. My "cell" is a square box of a bedroom with a twin bed up against one wall. There is no carpeting and only one window.

Escape is the first thought I have once I'm left alone. When I pull back the drapes, though, I find nothing but darkness. It's not because it's still night. The window is boarded up securely. And the room is locked, as well. In fact, it is re-locked every time someone ventures in.

So far, however, I've been lucky. My only visitor thus far has been Justin.

I suspect things will soon change.

In any case, the first night in my bedroom/prison cell, I can't sleep at all. I keep expecting the doorknob to turn, and for Dawson or Pierson to enter.

But nothing like that happens. Thank God.

The next day Justin brings breakfast, and later on, dinner. He is my way of keeping track of the days since I have no clock and the room is always artificially lit by a lamp.

Night number two, I am utterly exhausted. My body gives out and I sleep soundly in the little twin bed, my body pressed up against the cool wall. I'm so out of it that when Justin arrives with day three's breakfast of dried toast and juice, he can't get me up.

Only when he turns on the lamp, and yells, "Come on, Essa, get up!" do I throw off the covers and jump to my feet.

"Dammit, you scared me," I complain, sighing as I feel for and take a seat on the edge of the bed.

"Sorry," Justin replies. "I was worried Pierson was nearby."

I run my hand through my messy hair and wave him off. "It's okay. I'm just a big, emotional mess right now."

"No wonder, Essa," he says sadly.

He sits down next to me and offers me the tray of food. "You should eat," he urges.

"Yeah, I guess you're right." I move the tray to my lap, pick up a piece of toast, and take a bite.

While I eat breakfast, Justin appraises me, taking in the fresh sweatshirt and clean pair of jeans I changed into yesterday evening. Yeah, my first act of defiance was to remain in the coffee and bloodstained green work shirt and dirty jeans I'd been wearing when abducted. But then I realized I was only punishing myself. So I relented and changed my clothes. I even made use of the tub in the tiny bathroom attached to my room, but I made sure to take a superfast bath.

"Glad to see you finally got out of those grimy clothes," Justin says, at last. "But, you do know there are pajamas over there. That'd be a much more comfortable outfit to sleep in."

He gestures to a pile of folded articles of clothing piled on the floor, clothes that were in the room when I arrived.

Scoffing, I say, "Are you kidding? No way am I ever sleeping in anything more revealing than this. What if Dawson or that awful Pierson decide to come in my room in the middle of the night?"

"I don't think jeans would really stop them," Justin mumbles.

I smack his arm. "Thanks, like I need a reminder of how vulnerable I am."

"Sorry," he says, for the second time today.

My appetite is lost, so I place the tray on the floor. "I have to get out of here, Justin." I wipe my mouth with the edge of my sweatshirt.

"I know, Essa, I know."

"So, what are we going to do?"

Lowering his voice, he says, "We keep things as planned. If things go like you think they will, you won't be a prisoner much longer."

Yesterday, when Justin brought in my meals, we discussed my situation, and how best to get out of it. I told him about Farren, and what he is capable of. After some heavy deliberation, we decided the best course of action—for now, and as long as Justin can keep me safe—is to wait for Farren to rescue me. But though things have been okay, so far, I know my situation could change at any time.

"We still need a back-up plan," I say. "What if Farren can't find me?"

"We'll think of something, then," he says.

"Like what?" I press.

Lifting his glasses and rubbing his eyes, he says, "I don't

know, Essa. Let me think on it some, all right?"

"Great," I say sourly. "Think on it, Justin."

"Hey." He nudges my arm. "No sad face. I'm sure I'll come up with something, Essa. I just need a little more time. I've been checking around the grounds, seeing what's out there, what we may have to deal with if we do get you out. Anyway, Dawson sent me out to buy more food and—"

"Wait, what?" I interrupt. "You've been allowed off the grounds by yourself?"

He nods slowly. "Um, yeah."

I lean back and look at him like he's crazy.

"Why haven't you just taken off?" I ask, stunned. "You should at least save yourself."

He touches my wrist. "Hey, I'm not leaving you. It's my fault you're trapped in this place. Plus, I made you a promise that I'd help you. I'm not going back on my word."

Our gazes meet, and I see the remorse and pain he feels. Justin regrets how his actions got me into this mess. But there's no use dwelling on what can't be changed.

"I appreciate it," I say, just above a whisper. "But if you were to decide to leave, I wouldn't be mad. I'd never blame you for getting out while you can."

"Don't be silly," he scoffs. And then, "Maybe I should try to find a pay phone next time Dawson sends me into town. The place is so old that I bet there are a few still standing. I could call 911 and—"

"No!" I cut him off. "That is *not* a good idea. If the police descend on this place—and they will if they know there's a kidnap victim up here—I'm as good as dead."

Justin blows out a breath. "I guess I didn't think it through."

"Hey." I touch his arm. "It was a good thought, though."

"Maybe it was," he says. "But not good enough."

I want to say, "We'll figure it out," but I'm not sure we ever will.

Anxious to change the subject, I say, "So, what does it look like out there? I couldn't see much the other night when we arrived. It was way too dark."

Justin scoots toward the wall and leans back against it. I do the same, our shoulders touching.

"There are a lot of woods out there," he says. "Really, like deep, deep forest. I think we could hide for a while if we could just get you out of this room."

"Yeah, good to know, just skip out of the room." I frown over at him. "And just how is *that* supposed to happen?"

"We'll think of something," he assures me. "There has to be something they missed."

He glances around, and I tell him, "I don't know, Justin. I've gone over every inch of this place…the little bathroom too…and I'm pretty certain there's no way out of here."

Undeterred by my pessimism, he stares over at the window. The drapes are closed, so before he gets too excited, I inform him, "It's completely boarded up. I checked, first thing the other day."

"How securely is it boarded?"

"Very. I tried pulling the wood off. Trust me that the window is not an option."

Still, Justin continues to stare over at the window, brow furrowed. "How thick can those wood boards be, Essa? It's just plywood, I'm sure. How hard did you try to get them off?"

"Pretty damn hard," I reply. "It's super secure. The wood must be steel-reinforced or something."

My first endeavors on day one was to search for easy ways out of this place—loose boards on the window, vents that could be pried open, weak walls to be broken through, *anything*. But after inspecting every nook and cranny, I found nothing that could be breached.

I tell Justin all of this, and then lament, "If we can't find a way out of here, I am so done."

"Don't give up hope," he says, smiling encouragingly.

He's turning out to be the hopeful one of the two of us. But, of course, he's not locked up all day and night. Nor does he face the specter of physical abuse…or worse.

Justin slides off the bed and walks over to the window. He pulls back the drapes and starts inspecting the boards.

"Has he been in to see you?" he quietly asks while tugging at each piece of wood, one by one.

I twist on the bed to face him, but he purposely keeps his body turned to the window.

"No," I sigh. "Not yet."

He means Dawson. We don't like to say his name, because we know when the visits from Dawson begin, things will get messy. If he doesn't get what he wants—apparently me hating Farren— the abuse will surely commence.

"Do you really think he'd put Pierson in here with me?"

I shudder at the thought, the vicious, hard eyes of Pierson haunting me.

"I don't know." Justin tugs harder at one particular board. He is worried for me. "I don't think we want to find out."

"Understatement of the year," I mumble.

Justin turns to me, finally. "Come here," he says. There's a fine sheen of sweat on his forehead and his soulful brown eyes behind the lenses of his glasses are aglow. He's really trying hard to help me.

Once I'm standing next to him, he places my hand on one of the boards. "Feel that?" he says.

At first, the board feels just as secure as the rest. But when I jiggle the slat of wood there is the tiniest bit of give.

"Justin!" I turn to him, renewed hope in my eyes...my heart...everywhere. "Oh, my God, it's loose. You pried it loose. I can't believe it."

Smiling, he replies, "I think we just found your way out."

"Damn, you are awesome."

I give him a quick hug, and then we start to work on uncovering the window, the metaphorical door to my freedom. We don't get far; a sharp rap on the door puts an end to any real effort. For now.

Justin and I scamper to the bed, and as I take a dutiful seat on the edge, he picks up the tray from the floor. "Who is it?" he calls out.

Pierson, his voice a booming bass, yells in, "Boss wants to see you *now*. Make it quick. He has an errand for you to run."

"I better go," Justin says to me under his breath.

"What kind of errands does Dawson send you on, anyway?" I ask, curious.

Adjusting his glasses, he replies, "Just what I told you, to the convenience store to pick up food and stuff."

"And then they let you make the food?" I nod to the tray. "Like, toast the bread, pour the juice."

"Yes," he confirms.

An idea comes to me. "Maybe you can sneak a knife in here. You know, in case one of them"—I nod to the door—"decides to pay me a visit."

"I would," Justin replies remorsefully. "But 'one of them' is always watching me when I prepare your food."

"Oh, okay." I'm sure I sound as dejected as I feel.

Jerking his chin to the window, he says, "Are you going to work on that while I'm gone?"

"Are you kidding?" I snort. "I doubt I'll do much else."

Justin stares at the window contemplatively. Pierson knocks again, impatient, and Justin grinds out, "Would you hold on a minute, for Christ's sake."

When he then steps over to the window, I ask, "What are you doing, Justin? You better hurry before Pierson wonders the same thing and barges in."

The last thing I want is for Pierson to find my window to freedom.

"I know." Justin draws the drapes closed. "Just covering up what we're doing."

I nod. "Oh, good thinking."

"We can't get caught, Essa." Justin's tone is dour. "Dawson will punish us severely."

I don't want to find out what "severely" might mean to a sicko such as Dawson, so gulping down the lump that forms in my throat, I assure Justin, "I'll be careful."

Another sharp rap on the door ends our discussion.

"Come on, dude," Pierson yells in. "What are you doing in there, anyway? If you touch the pussy before the boss gives the go ahead, he will kick your ass." He pauses, and oh-so-thoughtfully adds, "Hell, *I'll* kick your ass."

The thought of Justin and me secretly messing around behind Dawson's back is laughable. We look at each other and smile.

"He's an idiot," I whisper.

"Definitely," Justin replies.

A key slips into the lock, a soft grind, and I hurriedly say, "Shit! Go, Justin, go, hurry, before he comes in. That's the last thing we want."

"I'm outta here," Justin assures me as he rushes to the door.

He makes it before Pierson comes in, but the big creep does stick his head in when Justin opens the door to leave. Pierson levels me with a hard stare, and then does one of those I'm-watching-you movements, his fingers pointed to his eyes, then to me.

Whatever, creep.

After Justin leaves, along with Pierson, I work on one thing and one thing only—the loose board on the window. I find though it's not as tightly secured as the others, especially since Justin pried it loose some, it's still nailed on the window frame pretty damn solidly. As a result, my progress is minimal.

I don't give up, however. No freaking way. I keep pulling and shaking and pushing with everything I've got. That is, until I hear a key sliding into the lock.

Then, I stop everything.

"Shit." I quickly close the drapes and race back over to the bed, where I hurriedly plop down on the edge.

I'm hoping it's just Justin with dinner, since several hours have passed since he left.

Unfortunately, it's not Justin.

With a wicked smirk plastered on his face, Dawson steps into my room.

CHAPTER ELEVEN

Farren

RICK and I set up a point of operations at a rustic motor lodge about a mile down the hill from the ski lodge. It's one of about five establishments in town. The closest establishment to the motor lodge is a rundown convenience store, and a little farther down the road, an old-style gas station, with pumps that aren't even digital.

I send Rick to both establishments to pick up any security tapes they may have in their possession. There's a good chance one of the men holding Essa up at that damn lodge stopped in for provisions, or to fuel up the vehicle.

I don't like not knowing who we may be dealing with when we cobble together our rescue attempt. In this particular case, more so than any other ever before, failure is *not* an option.

So Room 105 in the motor lodge becomes our temporary home. In a room that sports a seventies gold and green motif with big concentric circles on the wallpapered walls there are two full-sized beds, a small desk, and an attached bathroom. It's not much, and it's outdated as hell, but the joint has Wi-Fi, so it will do.

Rick leaves to check on the security footage, and I set up my laptop on the desk. I attach a portable printer, and then, since there's not much to do at the moment, I try to rest for a few minutes, just to recharge.

I lie down on one of the beds, but I'm far too worried to relax. Closing my eyes for about ten minutes is the best I can do.

Then, I am back at the desk.

Grabbing up one of several burner phones Rick and I brought, I call Vincent down in DC.

"There's nothing new," he informs me as soon as he picks up. Vincent is not one for formalities, not that I give a shit.

"Okay," I reply. "I didn't think there'd be anything new, but I had to check."

"Hey, I get it," he replies. "No need to explain." Vincent knows how I feel about Essa, and he adds, "I'm really sorry this is happening, man."

"Yeah, thanks." I clear my throat. "Back to the business at hand..."

"Yeah?"

"I received the map you sent earlier and the layout of the old ski lodge. I have a few connections up in this area, and I know a reliable guy with a helicopter. I'm thinking if Rick and I rappelled from the copter onto the main lodge property, we could possibly enter the place through one of the heating vents up on the roof."

"That might work," Vincent says, his tone contemplative. "You'd be close enough to the chalet they're holding Essa in to have the element of surprise on your side."

"Yeah," I agree, "we would have that."

"What're you thinking, Shaw?" Vincent asks. "You sound hesitant."

"I want to go in as soon as possible, that's true," I begin. "But there is something holding me back."

"Not knowing who the other man is?" Vincent correctly guesses.

"Yes."

"There's another potential problem, too," he adds wearily.

"Aw, fuck. What now?'

"Any rescue-by-copter attempts have to be put on hold."

Rubbing the back of my neck, I wonder aloud, "Why's that?"

"I'm looking at the weather reports right now, and heavy rains are moving into your area. Visibility is going to be for shit for flying, especially up in those mountains."

I know he's right, and I mutter the one word that sums it up perfectly: "Fuck."

Making matters worse, when I get off the phone, Rick returns, but he's empty-handed.

"No security cameras at the gas station?" I ask.

He closes the door behind him with a thud. "Not a single one."

Goddammit, nothing is going right today. "What about the convenience store?" I lean back in the desk chair.

"No cameras in there, either. Guy at the station told me there's not much use for security measures up here."

"Makes sense," I say, running my hand through my hair in exasperation. "There's hardly any business, I'm sure there's no crime."

"Except for Dawson," Rick mutters.

I snort, "You got that right."

"Anyway," Rick says, "all was not lost. I did find out something that might be of interest, something we can pursue."

I raise a brow. "Some intel on the third man, hopefully."

"No, nothing on him." Rick shakes his head as he takes off his jacket. I notice the cotton is wet, making it look black instead of navy. The rain has arrived early, thus ensuring the setback Vincent predicted.

Rick tosses his jacket to one of the beds and it lands with a soggy thud. "So, anyway, here's what I got. The lady working at the convenience store was quite the talker. It seems since business is so slow up here, she makes it her personal mission to remember every face of every person that ventures in the store for anything."

"Oh?" My interest is piqued.

"Yep," Rick replies. "And, she was only too happy to describe the only customer to come in the past day or so."

"Yeah, so…?"

"Let's just say the guy she described bears an uncanny resemblance to someone we'd like to get our hands on to talk to."

I know the guy isn't going to be Dawson, there's no way he'd leave the resort property and take a chance on Essa getting away. It has to be the unknown guard…or the prick who got over on Essa.

"Justin," I say, guessing the prick.

"Red hair, glasses, a thin build… What do you think, Farren?"

"That's him."

"He's been in the store twice," Rick adds.

I want my hands on that kid. Rick may have to keep me from

killing him, but if I can hold my ire at bay long enough to get him to talk, we may get the intelligence we need to make our move.

"Farren," Rick prompts. "What are you thinking? Where do you want to go from here?"

Standing, I say, "Let's go pick him up. He's been in the store twice, you said. He's bound to come back sometime, right?"

Rick nods. "Probably, I would guess. But you should stay here, in case any intel comes in."

I sit back down. "Yeah, you're right."

Rick heads to the door, saying over his shoulder, "If I get him and bring him back, promise me you won't kill the kid."

That's a promise I begrudgingly make.

CHAPTER TWELVE

Essa

DAWSON enters my cramped room with bravado. I rise from the bed and nervously nod his way. It's then I notice he has a folder stuffed with papers in his hand.

Damn, what is the jerk up to now?

"Essalin, dear, how are you faring this fine day?" Dawson stops when he's halfway to me.

I hate that he sounds concerned. It's another lie; he couldn't care less for my well-being.

When I shrug, his eyes snap in anger. "Are your accommodations not to your liking?" He gestures around the room. "We could take the bed away if you prefer sleeping on the hard floor."

I bite my lip, resisting the urge to utter a smartass retort. Instead, I lie. "Everything is fine, actually."

"Comfortable?"

"Yes, very." Another lie.

He doesn't expect a truthful answer. Dawson is taunting me. If playing along allows him to lower his guard, however, it'll be well worth it.

"Good, good. That's what I like to hear." He adjusts his tie, crimson red, like blood, and then clears his throat.

Dawson is wearing a suit, like always. This one is dark brown and made of corduroy. An odd choice for summertime, but whatever, he is a weird dude. Still, he's not to be underestimated. With his hawk-like nose and beady eyes, he looks like a predatory falcon. And I know from personal experience he is just as ruthless.

After a surveying glance here and there, thankfully with no lengthy perusal of the curtained window, his gaze falls to me. I'm wearing jeans and a sweatshirt, same outfit as earlier, but he stares at my body like I'm in lingerie.

"I have to say, you're looking quite lovely today," he remarks.

"Thank you," I reply, cringing.

It's best to appease him, I tell myself. Still, when he takes a step toward me, I can't help but stumble back toward the bed.

"I'm not going to hurt you," he says, his voice filled with false kindness.

"Yeah, right," I snort.

He stops, frowning. "This can be easy, Miss Brant, or it can be made to be very difficult. The choice is yours."

I can't look at him. He's still a few feet away, but every alarm bell goes off in my head, warning me to get away.

"What do you want from me?" I murmur as I take another step back. My knees hit the edge of the bed. Shit, I'm trapped, and at Dawson's mercy. *Dear Lord.*

Dawson takes another step in my direction, and I sit down

on the bed, scoot back to the wall. I don't know if a bed is the safest place to cower in fear with this animal in the room, but I need as much distance as possible between us.

"Why do you fear me, Essa?" Dawson taunts. "I only wish to come a little closer to you in order to talk."

"What do you want to talk about?" My voice shakes, revealing my terror.

"Calm down," he orders, tapping the folder against his leg in agitation. "I want to show you some things, and I need for you to pay close attention."

"Okay."

"I also want you to be honest with yourself once you see what I have to show you."

I nod. "Yes, okay, I will."

Dawson moves back slightly. I guess to ease my fear. He continues to walk backwards, until he reaches the wall across from me. As he leans back against the peeling plaster, I relax slightly.

Still, he chastises me. "Oh, Essa, really now… Do we need such unnecessary drama?" He makes a tsking sound. "After all, I am not the man you should fear."

I don't respond. I know he means I should fear Farren. How ridiculous. But Dawson won't be happy till I hate the man I love.

Why, though?

"Why does it matter so much to you that I love Farren?" I boldly inquire.

"Because I have something I'd like to ask of you. And you can't make a proper decision, or provide me with an answer, until you know all the facts. You are currently too blinded by love."

Hmm…I'm curious. What game is Dawson playing? I can't

help but stare at him with curiosity.

"Ah, I have your interest piqued. That's a start."

"I don't know what you want from me," I say, "but I can tell you right now that I will never hate Farren."

"We'll see about that," he growls as he withdraws a stack of papers from the folder.

He steps forward and holds a page out to me. I lean forward, take it. Then I sit back just as swiftly.

Staring down at the paper in my hand, I determine it's a copy of a newspaper clipping—some diplomat in a third-world country was shot recently. Coincidentally, it's the same third-world country Farren was in last week.

"So?" I say.

Dawson nods to the clipping. "Read it, please."

"I see the headline," I snap. "A diplomat was shot in another country."

"A country Farren Shaw was visiting."

"Yes, I know. What's that have to do with him, though?"

"It has everything to do with your boyfriend, Miss Brant." Dawson takes a menacing step toward the bed. "It was Farren who killed that man."

I scoff, "Yeah, right. Farren was in that country helping his dad."

"Is that what he told you?"

"Yes."

Dawson chuckles. "Farren is not who you think he is."

"I know him better than you do," I retort.

And that is what finally sets him off.

Without warning, Dawson throws the folder at me. Papers and photos flutter all over and around the bed. Two pictures land on the blanket in front of me, and I can't help but look down.

I gasp. One photo depicts a bloody body, gender undistinguishable. The other photo is of a man, dead, a huge bullet hole wound in his head.

"Farren lied to you," Dawson hisses. "He lies to you all the time. You don't know what he does when he goes away. *This* is what he does, Essa. He keeps secrets, big secrets. Does that sound like something a man who supposedly loves you would do?"

"Shut up," I cry. "I don't want to know any more."

Despite my words, I can't help but stare down at the strewn papers and pictures. I pick up a single page. It's a communication marked classified, a confirmation of an assassination. There's a photo to the left that then catches my eyes, a picture of a man with his head blown clean off.

I push the photo away, and it flutters to the floor. "Just go away," I plead.

If Farren did indeed kill these men, then there must have been a reason. These men must've been bad guys.

Dawson, quick to gather where my thoughts are heading, says, "Enemies of the state, that's what your government chooses to call these men." He throws his hands up in the air. "But who decides such things, Miss Brant? Would *you* act on someone else's word? Would you *kill* someone just because you were ordered to?"

"Who ordered Farren to kill these men?" I whisper. "Who does he work for?"

"Same people as before," Dawson replies.

"He's out of Special Forces," I maintain.

I'm confused, and Dawson jumps right on it. "That's exactly what Farren would like you to believe."

"Stop, please." I choke back a sob. "I don't want to hear anything else."

Dawson's not done. He goes in for the kill. "Have you ever heard of Black Ops, Essa?"

I nod my head once, and Dawson continues, "Some claim it's a made-up agency, but I assure you the Black Ops arm of the government is quite real. Those men in the photos would tell you the same…if they still could."

I try to reconcile what Dawson is saying with what I know of Farren. Finally, I say, "If those men were enemies of the state, they weren't good people."

As I speak, I am crying, crying because Farren kept all of this information from me. Why did he tell me he was done with his service to the country? Why would he lie to me?

Trying to rationalize all possibilities, I say, "Maybe Farren is in this Black Ops, okay. But if that's true, then maybe he just provides information to them, like intelligence—"

Dawson cuts me off. "Do you really believe that?" he asks softly.

"I don't know."

In a calm voice, too calm since he thinks he is winning, he says, "Let me assure you that Farren is not merely some intelligence agent. He's a sniper, Miss Brant, one of the best in the world."

"A sniper…"

As I trail off, Dawson smugly wants to know, "How does it feel to be lied to by someone you love?"

"I'm sure Farren had his reasons," I whisper.

"What reason could be good enough to not share his secrets with you, the woman he supposedly loves?"

I shrug. Yes, I'm hurt, but I don't know what Dawson expects from me. Does he really believe my love could so easily be turned? Love doesn't work that way. But he wouldn't know. Dawson has probably never loved anyone in his life. He's far too self-serving.

After watching me closely for a minute, he walks over to the bed and stops when he is in front of me. Jerking his chin to the mess he's made, he says, "Look over the papers. There are more. Your boyfriend, your lover," he sneers, "has tallied up an impressive kill total."

"I still don't know why you're telling me all this," I mutter. "What do you want from me?"

"I want only one thing." Dawson kneels down in front of me, like he's appeasing me, showing me how reasonable he can be. *Yeah, right.*

"What's the one thing you want?" I ask.

"I want you to help me get close to Farren, close enough to end his life. I want him to know before he dies that it was you who turned on him. It's my perfect revenge, to watch his reaction when he realizes the only woman he's ever loved has led him to his demise."

Dawson is truly crazy. I see it in his eyes. He's a monster, yes, but he's certifiable too. I have to play this thing carefully. Nothing could ever turn me against Farren, no matter how upset I am.

But to save my hide, and Farren's too, I nod appeasingly and tell Dawson what he wants to hear. "Okay, I promise I'll look over all this stuff. I'll keep an open mind to what you're saying."

Dawson's eyes widen, making him look like a startled owl. "And you'll consider my proposition?"

"Yes," I lie.

He stands, overjoyed, rubbing his hands together like the

villain he is.

"This is beautiful," he says. "And once you've seen things my way, you will agree, Miss Brant, that revenge is best served cold."

"I have no doubt," I say.

Of course, I fail to add the most important part: How sweet revenge will taste when I get out of this place and Farren ends Dawson…once and for all.

CHAPTER THIRTEEN

Farren

PICKING up Justin is easy. After all, it's not like the kid's a professional. Rick nabs him outside the convenience store and drags him back to the motor inn without incident.

"Step into the room slowly," I hear Rick order Justin as the door to our room swings open. No weapon is visible in Rick's hand, not that it would matter out here in no-man's-land, but I'm certain there's a gun pointed discreetly at Justin's back in the hand I can't see.

"Why are you doing this?" Justin asks.

His voice sounds level and firm, but when he comes into the room I see the abject fear in his eyes, even behind those glasses.

"Just keep moving," Rick mutters.

Justin continues into the room at a snail's pace, and Rick, seemingly at his wit's end with this rookie criminal, gives him a hard shove. Justin trips forward, right into my path.

106

"Whoa there, big fellow"—he is kind of tall—"hold up." I help steady him, and the minute he looks into my eyes, it's clear he knows exactly who I am.

"Farren," he says, stepping way the fuck back.

Essa must have told him about me. But why would she do that?

I eye him curiously. "So, what's a nice college student like you doing out here in the middle of nowhere?"

"Nothing," he declares with a shake of his head. "Nothing at all."

He moves farther away from me, and that's probably wise. A part of me wants to kick his ass for what he's gotten Essa into, and that may still occur, but for now I have to hold off. There's more happening here than what meets the eye, I'm sure of it.

The kid backs right into Rick, who shoves him toward me.

"Have a seat," I say, gesturing to the edge of the bed. "There's no use pretending. We know who you are and why you're up here in these mountains."

He sits on the bed, stares down at the floor. "What do you want from me?" he whispers.

I pull up a chair, spin it around, and take a seat across from him. "We have some things we need to ask you." Justin eyes the door, and I warn, "Don't even think about running."

"I-I'm not."

I can't help but chuckle. "Yeah, sure you're not."

Rick sits down on the edge of the other bed, mere feet away. He clears his throat, a reminder to Justin that there are two of us, and only one of him.

He gives up fighting and closes his eyes. "Okay, I'm ready to talk," he says.

"Wise choice," I tell him. And then we get down to business. "What's happening with Essa?" I ask. "We know she's up at the old resort. Is she being treated properly? Is she all right?"

After one long exhale, Justin opens his eyes and says, "Yes, she's okay, all things considered."

I have to be sure of one thing. "No one has touched her. Please tell me no one has laid a hand on her."

"Uh…" I stand menacingly, and he shakes his head with vigor. "No, no, not in the way you're thinking." I breathe a sigh of relief and sit back down.

Justin, shuddering, says, "Dawson hit her the first day, just a smack." I give him a look that could kill, and he quickly adds, "Not that what he did was all right, but it wasn't a punch. She had a red mark, but she's okay now." Not meeting my eyes, he says, "Uh, nobody has, um, touched her in any way you might be thinking."

"For now," Rick interjects, and I shoot him a harsh look. "Sorry," he mutters.

I'm glad Essa has been left alone, but I am angry that Dawson dared to smack her. *Fucker*. He will pay for that.

I turn to Justin, my ire redirecting to the person responsible for Essa having been taken in the first place. "We wouldn't even be having this conversation if you hadn't tricked her into coming with you," I grind out through clenched teeth.

I glare at him until he flinches and looks away. "I'm sorry for my involvement," he murmurs. "I truly am."

I can't tell if he's bluffing. Either he's truly repentant, or he's a really good actor. It had better be the former, for his sake.

"In any case," I continue, "Essa won't be fine for long. Not with Dawson up there. It's only a matter of time before he hurts her." Justin doesn't disagree, and I add, "We need to get her out of there as soon as possible. Unfortunately, if Rick and I just drive up there and rush in, Dawson will kill Essa as revenge."

The kid swallows hard, Adam's apple bobbing. "I know," he says. "Essa said the same thing."

Aah, interesting. "So, you two have opportunities to talk."

"Yes." Justin perks up. "Dawson has me bringing her food every morning and every evening. That's why I was at the store. I was picking up bread and packaged cold cuts so I could make some sandwiches."

So, Justin has access to Essa. It makes me curious about something else. "How much time do you get alone with Dawson?"

Justin looks at me warily. "Not much. He's mostly with Pierson."

"That's the name of the guard up there?"

"Yes."

I look over at Rick. "Have you heard of him?"

He nods. "Yeah, he's in our files on Dawson. He's low-level, a guard, tough as nails, but not real smart. He'd not be much of a problem for you or me, but he could pose a threat to Essa."

"Great," I sarcastically mutter.

Rick doesn't need to come out and state that "a threat to Essa" is essentially his nice way of saying Pierson is a sick pervert, not unlike most of Dawson's handpicked cohorts. He will likely make a move on Essa.

"We need to get her out of there as soon as possible," I declare.

I motion to Rick, and he hands me a tiny device no bigger than a bean.

"This is a GPS tracker," I explain to Justin as I hold the tiny device out to him. "We need for you to find a way to plant it on

Dawson, and you need to do it soon."

"W-w-what?" Justin shies away from the device in my hand. "How in the hell am I supposed to pull off something like that?"

"You'll figure it out." I wave the device, and Justin eventually, albeit reluctantly, takes it.

I show him the tiny on and off switch at the base. "When you activate the tracker," I explain, "it will go live. We'll see this on our monitors, and then we'll know you've been successful."

"Why do you need for me to do this?" Justin asks, perplexed. "You know where he is. Just go in and get him."

"I told you we can't do that," I say, irritated. "Do you want Essa to end up dead?"

"Of course I don't," Justin replies.

His emotions betray him—the kid really cares for Essa. Who knew? An interesting development, for sure.

"Listen," I say, a bit more kindly now that I know he is sympathetic to Essa. "Dawson won't stay at the resort much longer. There's a helicopter landing pad behind the main lodge. I suspect that's how he got in, Pierson, too. Anyway, he will surely leave the same way." Sighing, I add, "And, Justin, I can't take the chance of him taking off and our losing track of Essa. You *have* to find a way to plant the device on him."

Justin stares down at the tracker in his hands. "Okay," he says, "I'll figure something out."

"Good."

He looks up at me and mutters cryptically, "Who knows? Maybe we will be out of there before he leaves and tries to take Essa with him."

Hmm, the kid is up to something. Rick and I exchange glances, and I say, "What exactly does that mean?"

"I don't expect you to believe me," Justin begins, "but I've been helping Essa. There's a boarded-up window in her room. We thought it was completely secure, but earlier today we discovered one of the boards is loose. If we pry all of them off, the window is big enough that I can get Essa out."

"Okay, even if that works," Rick interjects, "what's the plan from there?"

Justin turns to face Rick. "She and I make a run for it. It's all woodsy up there, down here, too. There are lots of places to hide on the way to town. In fact, I bet we could make it down to this motor lodge on foot."

I look over at Rick and say, "This could work."

He nods. "Yeah, it might be our best chance of getting Essa out of that place unharmed."

It's a good plan, better than nothing, but I still can't take the chance of Dawson taking off and not knowing when or where he'll strike next. "I still need you to plant that device," I say to Justin.

"Okay," he replies, nodding. "I'll do what I can."

With that decided, I boot up the laptop and start pulling up maps of the area. Justin and Rick gather round as I point out the best route for him and Essa to take if they get out of the chalet.

"This trail…" I point to a topography image on the screen. "You can see it's not as overgrown as some of the others. Plus, it starts near the back of the chalet. Look here…" I trace the route down the hill. "See, the trail heads straight into town."

"We'd come out by the service station," Justin muses as he peers at the screen. "That's just down the road from here."

"Stay away from the main road, though," Rick cautions. "If you make it that far, keep behind the buildings."

"Yes, of course. We will."

Once everything is set, Rick returns Justin to the store. When he comes back to the motor lodge, he asks, "Do we fully trust this kid?"

"What choice do we have?" I reply, sighing. "I think he's our best option."

"Yeah, you're probably right."

I bite out a humorless laugh. "Hell, I better be more than 'probably' right."

Rick shrugs, but he's careful how he answers. Keeping it vague, he mutters, "Like you just said, it's the only viable option."

I nod in agreement, but all I can think is this Justin-kid better not double-cross us.

If he does, there will be no mercy on my part.

CHAPTER FOURTEEN

Essa

JUSTIN is late with my dinner, so I pace around the tiny room I am forever trapped in. A bit dramatic, but it sure feels like I've spent an eternity here.

When Justin finally arrives, I rush over to him. "Oh, thank God," I gush.

The door is barely closed, and I should be more careful, but I can't help myself.

"Where have you been, anyway?" I say. "I was really worried. There's no clock in here, but I know it has to be close to midnight."

"Essa, be quiet," Justin snaps.

I frown as he sets the tray he's holding—a dinner of soup and a cold sandwich—on the floor. "You can't go off like that when I'm barely in your room. What if Pierson was close by, like down the hall?"

He's right, and I apologize. "I'm sorry. You're right. I'm just on edge, that's all."

"Why?" Justin asks. "Did something happen?"

Quietly, I reply, "Dawson paid me a visit."

"Shit." Justin sits down on the edge of my bed. He takes his glasses off and rubs his eyes. "I'm afraid to ask, but I have to. What did he want?"

I step over to the bed. "He wanted what he's wanted from the start—for me to turn against Farren. Now, he expects me to lure him into a trap so he can kill him."

"Jesus."

"Oh, and the best part," I continue, "Farren gets to die knowing I double-crossed him."

Justin slips his glasses on and mutters, "Dawson is fucking delusional."

"You think?" I walk over to the window and pull back the drape. "It might not matter, though. Look over here. I've been working all evening on this, and the loose board is even looser."

"Good, we have to get you out of here as soon as we can."

Justin sounds anxious, and I know he's holding something back. "What is it?" I ask.

He clears his throat, looks over at me. "Okay, if I tell you what happened when I was in the town, promise me you'll stay calm."

I move to the bed and sit down next to him. "Look at me." I motion to my face. "I'm as calm as can be."

"Essa," he chastises. "This isn't funny."

Sighing, I say, "I know. It's just been a stressful day, like I said. I think my brain is fried."

"It's okay," Justin says, and then he blurts out, "So, your boyfriend's friend, some guy named Rick, grabbed me at the convenience store." I gasp, shocked, but Justin speaks right over me. "Listen, Essa. Farren is in the town, okay. But you need to stay calm. He and this Rick guy are holed up at a motor lodge, but—"

"What?" I cut him off. "Farren is less than a mile away and he's not up here saving me?"

"Yes, he's close. But he can't make a move, not yet. Dawson will…you know…"

He looks away, and I finish for him. "Dawson will kill me if he thinks there's no way out for him."

"Yeah," Justin says softly, "that's what Farren said to me."

Sighing, I concede, "He's right. Nothing has really changed"

I stare down at my hands clasped in my lap. Farren is so close, yet so far. I wonder if he feels as trapped by these circumstances as I do.

Justin, noticing my downcast eyes, says, "Hey, look, there's still a plan in place, but it's better than ours."

"There's a new plan?"

"Yes." He smiles kindly. It's the smile that endeared him to me in the early days at the coffee shop. "I told Farren and his friend about the loose board on the window. I told them about our plan to escape. Farren thinks it's the best option at this point. The only change is if we can get out of here unnoticed and make it through the woods, we can meet up with them at the motor lodge."

"That's better than just running," I reply excitedly. "I was worried about where we'd go after we got out of here." I sigh. "That is, if we really do escape."

"We will," Justin assures me.

He's so confident that it renews my faith. We need all the positivity we can get if we're going to pull this off.

But then he says, "There's just one more thing," and my heart

115

sinks a little.

"Oh no… What is it?"

Justin leans forward and pulls a tiny device from the back pocket of his jeans. "This," he states as he holds a little black object aloft. "I'm supposed to plant this thing on Dawson."

"What is it?" I ask.

He hands it to me. "It's a GPS device, a tracker."

"It looks so simple," I examine the smooth black outer casing and the tiny switch at the base.

"Hey, don't activate it," Justin says when he sees my finger hovering around the switch.

"I wasn't going to turn it on," I tell him.

I move my finger away from the switch, just to be sure there's no accidental activation. "What happens when it's activated?" I whisper.

"When I turn it on it will send a signal to Farren that the device is planted on Dawson. And, from that point on, Farren can track Dawson's every movement."

"I don't know, Justin," I say, hedging. "This is great and all, if it works, but I don't see how you'll ever get close enough to Dawson to plant it on him."

Justin muses, "Hmm, I thought that, too. But I'm thinking if I can slip it in a pocket of one of his suits—"

"Yeah, right," I snort. "Do you have access to his room? That's where he keeps his suits, I'm sure."

"No."

"Well, he never takes off whatever suit jacket he's wearing, and he'll wonder if you try to get close to him to plant that thing."

"True," Justin agrees.

But then, inspiration strikes. "Hey, I have an idea," I say. "I bet *I* could get close enough to Dawson to plant the tracker on him."

Justin stands and starts pacing around my tiny room, much like I was doing earlier.

He shakes his head. "No way, Essa, that is way too dangerous. You'd have to get pretty damn close to slip that little thing in his pocket. And he'd have to be completely distracted."

"Yep, he would need to be distracted," I agree, my voice soft. "But it can be done."

Justin slows to a stop and turns to me. He knows what I'm thinking. I can distract Dawson if I come on to him.

"Have you lost your mind?"

I stand and go to him. "It's a good plan, Justin," I say, pleading my case. "It could work."

"And what happens when you hit on him, Essa? How are you going to stop things from going too far?"

I shrug. "I don't know. I'll figure that out when, and if, it comes to that."

"It *will* come to that."

"I can't worry about it now," I state, determined. "We have to plant the tracker, right?"

"Yeah, but…" Justin, seeing how determined I am, switches tactics. "Farren wouldn't want you to do this, Essa. He asked *me* to plant the device. I should be the one to do it."

Frustrated, I hold the GPS out to him. "Fine, take it. You'll probably get us both killed, but, hey, we'll probably end up dead anyway."

Justin blows out a frustrated breath, but he doesn't take the device from me. He knows I'm right. If he gets caught planting that thing, we are as good as dead.

"I'm sorry," I say, "but I really think my plan is our only option."

He says nothing, and just when I think my ally and I have reached an impasse, he relents. "Okay, but promise me you'll not take any crazy chances. If it's too risky, just hold off. We'll find another way."

I nod in agreement, but there's no way I'm backing out now. Justin will never get close enough to Dawson.

Either I get it done, or I die trying.

CHAPTER FIFTEEN

Farren

WITH the wheels in motion—we're waiting for Justin to plant the tracker and for him to get Essa out of the chalet—there is nothing to do but wait at the motor lodge. Down time, I hate it.

"This fucking sucks," I gripe to Rick after a couple of days of the same routine—me seated at the desk, watching the monitor on the laptop, waiting for shit to happen, while my partner lounges on the bed.

I don't know how much longer I can take it. I am not a patient man by nature, particularly not when I'm so close to Essa I can almost taste her. I urge myself to remain calm, though. Pinching my nose, I close my eyes. And then I'm back on task—staring at the computer screen, like I do most hours of the day. I'm waiting for the GPS activation light to turn from red to green, which will indicate Justin has been successful in planting the tracker.

"Yeah, the waiting sucks balls," Rick agrees from where he is leaned back against the headboard. He's flipping TV channels, remote in hand.

I nod, just as he finds something watchable.

"The Yankees are playing," Rick says, gesturing to the TV. He turns up the volume. "Want to watch the game for a while? Let me take a turn at staring at that screen. You've been at it all day."

Sighing—hell, there's nothing happening anyway—I reply, "Yeah, sure."

Rick stands and tosses me the remote. Just as I catch it, his cell phone buzzes, moving across the nightstand next to the bed.

Picking up his phone, he glances at the screen. "It's Haven," he announces. "She's probably checking in again."

My sister calls often, Rick more than me. Sometimes she calls my cell, but I think it's only when Rick is unavailable. Rick is the one who soothes her, calms her frazzled nerves. Like all of us, Haven is a wreck while we wait for shit to go down.

"I'm going to take this out there." Rick motions to the door.

"Yeah, okay, fine."

Fuck the game. I remain at the computer. But as the tracker activation indicator stays red, I find myself muttering to the screen, "Come on, Justin."

Ten minutes pass, and still nothing happens. Except that Rick returns from outside where he took his call.

"Haven hanging in there at the apartment?" I ask.

"Yeah,"—he nods—"she's good. Doesn't like the guard you placed there, though. She says he's not much of a talker." I laugh. "But besides that, things are cool."

Leave it to Haven to grumble about the guard's conversation skills. I'm sure she'd have much preferred I allowed Rick to stay in the city with her. But he's far too skilled for babysitting duty. I need Martinez here.

When I turn back to glance at the screen the indicator light starts flashing, erratic little blips that garner my full attention. "Hey," I say, "I think we may have something here."

Rick steps over to the desk, just as three quick *bleeps* emit from the speaker. The tracker icon finally turns green.

"We're live," I announce, scrubbing my hands down my face in relief.

"Finally," Rick mutters.

I'm relieved as hell that things are moving along, but I'm nervous as well, for the same reason. Things are finally rolling, yes, but I need Essa the fuck out of that place in order to truly relax.

"The kid actually came through," Rick muses. He sounds surprised. Guess he had even less confidence than I did that Justin would be successful in planting the device on Dawson.

"Yeah, it appears he did," I reply.

Rick then asks, "Do you think Justin can get Essa out of there before Dawson takes off with her?"

I lean back in the desk chair. "Jesus, I sure as hell hope so."

Unfortunately, hope is all I have at this point. And I hate it. I hate that Essa's fate is in someone else's hands. Once she's out of there, however, all that will change. I'm not letting her out of my sight until Dawson is eliminated.

And this time, there will be no slipping away, no escape on his part. I have the tracker on the bastard; his ass is mine.

CHAPTER SIXTEEN

Essa

WITH the decision made that I am the best man—or woman, as it were—for the operation of planting the device on Dawson, I am set to wait for the perfect opportunity. But then Justin insists we should hold off until we've made more progress on the window.

"We have to wait until our escape route is ready," Justin says the night we agree on me planting the device.

"But what if the best chance comes before then?" I inquire.

"Essa, just wait," Justin replies, his tone weary. "If Dawson finds the device and we're still in this place, we're dead."

He has a point, so I relent.

As a result, we spend the next couple of days pulling and prying at the remaining boards on the window. Justin helps when he brings in my meals, but mostly it is up to me.

And this is where things stand two days later. The original

loose board isn't completely off, but it's dislodged. It's about ready to go, I know it, which lends an air of extra importance in keeping it covered with the drapes, particularly when Dawson visits. And that is, these days, unfortunately, often.

"Have you thought about my proposal?" Dawson asks during this day's late afternoon visit. "Will you help me get to Farren?"

The man is persistent as hell. "I'm thinking about it," I lie.

"You've gone through all the information in the file I left for you, yes?" I nod. "You see Farren is no better than what you think of me."

I shrug. "Yeah, I guess so." *Another lie.*

Dawson is delusional if he thinks leafing through the pages of information he left could ever turn me against Farren. And, yes, I did read *everything*. I looked at all the disgusting photos, too, images of corpses, depictions of violence.

One thing I can't deny is that Farren is efficient as hell. And he's definitely a sniper, a very good one, it would seem. He kills when ordered to, but I don't know who does the actual ordering. There's no name for the agency he reports to. I've concluded it appears to be what Dawson said it was—a branch of Black Ops.

So, does all this newfound knowledge make me think differently about the man I love? Absolutely not. I love Farren, good and bad. That's what love is. You can't dictate what your heart feels, not that I'd care to try.

"You feel differently about Farren now?" Dawson presses.

I can't disclose my true feelings to Dawson, so I shrug and say, "I don't know for sure, but I think I am seeing him in a different light, now that I've seen all the proof of the stuff he's done."

"I knew you'd see things my way," Dawson says smugly. "You realize now he has lied to you?"

"Yes."

"So, do you see how *my* vengeance could be yours, as well? When Farren Shaw realizes you led me to him, a part of him will die before I even kill him."

I hate Dawson. It takes every ounce of strength to nod and smile.

"Excellent," Dawson says, "excellent, Miss Brant. I'm so pleased by and impressed with you." He turns to where I'm standing by the bed and takes a step toward me. I have to resist the impulse to cower away. Remember, I have a task to complete.

In my hand, hidden in my grasp, lies the tiny GPS device. This could be my only opportunity to plant the damn thing on Dawson. He's wearing one of his signature suits, and I notice it has several pockets.

Perfect.

"You're not afraid of me, are you?" Dawson taunts as he comes closer.

"No," I reply, striving to keep my voice steady.

Another step closer and I switch on the device.

I imagine Farren down at the motor lodge, looking at the computer screen and seeing the device has been activated.

Damn, I can't fail now.

"You seem a bit nervous for someone who claims not to be afraid." He stops inches from me, cocking his head. "What are you hiding from me, Essalin?"

Oh, shit. "Nothing," I croak.

"Why do I not believe you?"

It's time to put on the show of my life.

Casting my eyes downward, I shift my weight, jutting my hip out. Flirtatiously, I say, "Maybe I am hiding something. I think

I've been too ashamed to admit it, to myself, and especially to you, but there is something."

His heavy brows shoot up. I have his full attention now. "Oh, and what could you possibly be ashamed to admit? Do tell."

Swallowing hard, I say as demurely as I can, "Do you remember that day at your compound out in the desert?"

Dawson adjusts himself, and I struggle not to puke. "Yes," he says gruffly. "I remember watching you come, Miss Brant. Bent over the hood of the car, you looked magnificent. Truth be told, I wanted to be the one with my fingers in your pussy, watching and feeling your juices flow down my hand."

Oh, God, I don't know if I can do this. But I must.

"I kind of wanted it to be you, too," I lie. "I'd never tell Farren, of course, but I liked you watching us. I liked you watching *me*. You should have joined in."

Dawson barks out a guffaw. "Your boyfriend would never have allowed such a thing."

I shrug. "Yes, you're probably right, but he's not here now."

This horrid man who I hate like no other narrows the gap between us in two seconds flat. His chest is inches from mine as he softly murmurs, "No, he is not."

I feel desire rolling off this repulsive man, and I want to run far, far away. But there's nowhere to go, and besides, I am in this now.

Do it, Essa, I imagine Farren saying. *Be brave, sweetheart.*

My palms feel sweaty, wet from fear. The device slips around in my grasp, but I don't dare drop it.

"Having second thoughts?" Dawson asks.

"No, no." I shake my head. "Just nervous, I guess."

He reaches out and caresses the side of my face, not unlike a cat toying with its prey.

"Don't be nervous," he says. "I'll go easy on you."

And then, before I can reply, his dry, leathery lips slam into mine.

Ugh. I have to kiss him back, to keep up my charade, but doing so is beyond disgusting. Dawson jams his tongue in my mouth and groans lustily. Meanwhile, his hand snakes up under my T-shirt, where he tugs roughly at one of my nipples through my bra. I act like I like it, and he lowers the cup and pinches. I long to slap his hand away, but I can't let him know my true emotions. I *have* to play the game.

Placing my hands at his waist, I let out a mewling sound to act as if I like his hands on me.

He deftly reaches behind my back and unclasps my bra, and with the fabric loosened, his hands are all over my breasts.

I think I'm going to vomit.

Rapidly, keeping my head in the game, I rub up and down the sides of his body, letting my knuckles graze over the pockets on either side of his suit jacket.

Now is the time.

Dawson starts making disgusting grunting noises in my mouth, before he pulls away and trails kisses down my neck. His hands remain under my shirt the whole time, manipulating my nipples, pinching and tugging. It becomes more and more uncomfortable, not arousing in any way. And it all feels so wrong. I almost back out, but then he moves us closer to the bed.

Time is running out. At this rate, he'll have not only my clothes off, but his own clothes gone, as well.

I need to move more quickly.

As covertly as possible, I slip the tracking device in to one of his suit jacket pockets, the one to his left. When the deed is done, I let out a sigh that Dawson mistakes for unbridled passion.

He stops kissing me, leans back slightly. "I knew you'd want this as much as me," he says, spit gathering at the corners of his mouth.

I smile, playing my role to the hilt. He grins back…but then his grin turns evil.

Roughly, and out of the blue, he shoves me down on the bed. "Time for the real fun to begin, Miss Brant," he says flatly.

"Um…"

Dawson growls, "Shut up, and get those clothes off."

I hesitate. What should I do? Take off my clothes? I can't do that. No way, not willingly. But how am I supposed to get out of this mess? Now that I've been successful in planting the device, I want nothing more than for Dawson to leave the room. I certainly don't plan to have any kind of sex with him. I'd rather die truth be told. Clearly, I need to find a way to hold off this madman.

"I'm waiting," he says, impatiently tapping his dress-shoe clad foot. "Or, are you having second thoughts?"

"Maybe we should wait," I mumble, looking down. "I'm suddenly not feeling very well."

At first, he doesn't respond, so I venture a glance up to his face.

And…shit…

Towering over me, Dawson looks angrier than I've ever seen him. His beady eyes are narrowed to thin slits.

"Get those fucking clothes off right now," he growls. "Or I assure you I will rip them off your body." Reaching forward, he grabs my chin and squeezes so tightly I'm sure I'll be left with a bruise. "I am not a man who plays games, Miss Brant," he warns.

"Do you understand?"

I nod, and he lets go of me, but not before giving me a final hard squeeze that just about numbs my jaw. So much for going easy on me, I should've known it would not be this man's way.

With emotion I can no longer hold back, I let out a choked sob. I am trapped, and if I continue to resist Dawson will hurt me, possibly beyond repair.

Defeated, I slip my T-shirt over my head.

"Hurry it along," Dawson orders when I fumble with slipping my bra straps off my shoulders.

Just as the last bit of fabric covering my torso falls away, exposing my breasts, Dawson unzips his fly. "Take off your jeans," he orders.

I pop the top button as tears slide down my cheeks, hot and wet. I am prepared for the worst—Dawson is going to fuck me. And it won't be nice. I think of Farren and my heart constricts. I am failing him in so, so many ways.

And then, in the middle of my reverie of regret, a knock on the door stops everything.

I freeze, while Dawson, annoyed, shouts over his shoulder, "Go the fuck away."

"Boss," the voice of Pierson rings out. "I'm sorry to bother you, but this is important."

"I said to leave me the fuck alone!" Dawson bellows.

I see his dick hardening in his pants, and I pray Pierson can convince him to leave.

Turning back to me, Dawson reaches forward to, I'm sure, rip away my jeans. But, again, Pierson distracts him, yelling in, "It's about the incoming helicopter. I think you'll want to hear this."

Helicopter, uh-oh. Good thing I planted the tracker on

Dawson. It looks like he is planning to move us to another location sooner than we thought.

Dawson huffs, annoyed, and then he barks at me, "Put your goddamn shirt and bra back on, you little tease. I'll deal with you later."

We'll see about that.

My breathing quickens to pants of relief. I've been granted a reprieve, and I can't get my jeans buttoned and my bra and tee back on fast enough.

Dawson watches me, and for a scared minute, I'm afraid he'll stay.

But he doesn't.

On his way to the door he stops and turns back to me. "I'll return soon, Miss Brant," he says. "And then, we're going to have lots of fun, you and me." It's clear in his eyes that he plans to finish what he started.

He winks, and I think, *Hell, no.*

I resist the urge to glance over at the window, the metaphorical door to my freedom. Behind the closed drapes lies my escape. And if all goes as planned, I will be long gone from this room before Dawson ever returns.

ONE hour of peace, one hour to pull myself together, and one hour to work on the window. Not three separate hours, no, one single hour in which to accomplish these things.

I figure it will take Dawson a minimum of an hour to check on the helicopter and return. I may actually have more time, he could come back way later, but I choose to err on the side of caution.

I have to get out of here.

If Dawson returns I cannot be with him, not in any way. Kissing him and having him grope me was my limit. I'd rather die than go further with him. He'll probably beat me into submission, though, and have his way with me. And then he'll whisk me away in the copter that's on its way.

God, I need to work faster.

With that in mind, I kneel on the floor and start yanking the hell out of the loose board. It feels so ready to go, just like earlier. Encouraged, I use the bed behind me for leverage, pulling at the board with all my might with my feet braced on the footboard.

Suddenly, a single loud popping noise shatters the silence. Three long-ass nails go flying, and I fly backwards, landing on my ass. "Ouch." I grimace.

But then I see what happened and I am smiling like a Cheshire cat.

The motherfucking board is off the window!

And not just off the window, it is in my hands. Dropping the wood slat to the floor, I crawl back over to the window and stare through a narrow slice of exposed glass.

Tears form in my eyes. I want to cry out in joy.

Oh, my God, the outdoors has never looked more appealing. It's early evening, and the sun is melting into the trees, dousing the tops like they're aflame. Well, my heart sure is aflame. I feel like running, jumping through the window. Freedom calls to me, beckoning me to find refuge away from Dawson deep in the surrounding forest.

I almost do it, too. I resist the urge to pull away the rest of the boards and run the hell away. But I have to wait for Justin. He stuck with me when he could have escaped any one of the times he was sent to town. It's my turn to come through for him. My goal is to have this window ready for the both of us to crawl through.

With a newfound urgency I get back to work. And, wow, was Justin ever right. With one board gone, the rest snap off easily. One by one, I toss nine wooden slats to the floor.

Our escape hatch is ready.

"Where is Justin, dammit?" I murmur to myself as I glance around my little room like he might magically appear.

If only.

"Damn, Justin, hurry it the hell up."

I don't have a clock, but since it's clear from angle of the setting sun that it's early in the evening, I expect Justin to arrive with my dinner any minute. But when some time passes and he doesn't show up, I have a horrible thought. What if Dawson returns first? The drapes won't hide what's been done to the window. Even though the sky is darkening, light is still filtering in, not to mention all the boards are scattered on the floor.

My short-lived joy turns to worry. Then, making matters worse, a key grinds into the lock on the door.

"No, no, no." I stand, turning left to right. There's nowhere to hide. I am so done.

In a state of panic—blood rushing in my ears, my pulse racing—I turn to the door and face my fate.

To my relief, though, a familiar voice rings out just as the door swings open. "Essa," Justin says quietly, "it's just me."

Ever since Dawson began visiting Justin has taken to announcing his arrival. I've never been so thankful to hear his voice. "Oh, thank God," I breathe out as I crumple to the edge of the bed to catch my breath.

I must look as frazzled as I feel, since Justin takes one look at me, and rushes over to kneel at my feet. "What the hell?" he mutters.

Balanced in his left hand is a plate with a huge sandwich. He places the plate on the floor so he can focus on me

"What happened?" he asks, his hands settling on my knees.

"I thought you were Dawson coming in again."

"Again?" His brow creases with worry. "He visited you today?"

I snort. "Doesn't he visit me every damn day?"

"Yeah, good point."

Justin looks me over, appraisingly, his gaze taking in the wrinkled lavender fabric of the tee hanging out over my jeans. "He didn't hurt you, did he?" he asks worriedly.

I shake my head. "No, not really, but I had to kiss him. And he did, uh, touch me some."

"Oh, Essa, I am so sorry."

"He only touched my chest," I hurriedly add. "Not that his hands on me at all wasn't awful. But, you know, nothing worse happened."

"I'm surprised he stopped," Justin says.

"Pierson inadvertently stopped him."

"How in the hell did *he* stop him?"

I explain everything that happened with Dawson, and how Pierson interrupted what was surely about to become a horrid assault. "Well, thank God you're okay," Justin says when I finish.

"You're not kidding."

Justin bites his lip, and then quietly says, "I hate to ask, but, were you able to plant the GPS?"

I nod. "Yes."

He closes his eyes. "Good, now we can get out of here."

Justin has been so concerned with what happened to me with Dawson that he hasn't even noticed the uncovered window. It's dark now, so no light is coming in, surely contributing to him missing what should be obvious.

I smile and say, "We should leave, like, immediately, I think." I gesture to the window.

"Shit, Essa." Justin jumps to his feet. "You've been busy since Dawson left you alone."

"I have. He was all the motivation I needed to work hard and fast."

Justin steps over a few of the strewn wood pieces and says, "I can't believe I didn't see this mess."

"You were worried about me."

He glances back at me. "I was."

Justin turns back to the window and adds, "You are so lucky Dawson didn't come back and see this."

"I know," I agree. "I pulled all the boards off after he left, and once the first one went, the rest followed. I was so worried you were him coming back."

Justin taps the glass lightly, his eyes on the outside world. "Did you say Pierson mentioned something about a helicopter coming in?"

"Yes." I go to Justin, put my hand on his shoulder. "We should definitely get out of here soon."

"No shit."

Justin raises the window, and I take a step back, overwhelmed. Fresh air never smelled so good. Closing my eyes, I breathe in the summer evening. But then a wave of dizziness comes over me, and I almost topple over.

"Hey, hey." Justin grabs my elbow. "Are you all right?"

"Uh-huh."

He retrieves the plate of food still by the bed. Walking back over to me, he picks up half of the big sandwich, waving it my way. "Here. You should eat before we go."

"I'm not really hungry," I protest, hand out.

"Come on." He presses the half-sandwich into my proffered hand. "Can't have you passing out in the woods, you know."

"True."

I try to take a couple of bites, but I'm far too anxious to consume more than a nibble.

"That's it?" Justin asks when I hand back what remains.

"I can't eat any more," I tell him as I struggle to swallow the final bite of bread and cold cuts. "I'm just too nervous to eat," I explain once I get it down.

Justin peers down at the sandwich hungrily, and I add, "Go ahead. You should have the rest."

"Are you sure?"

I nod, and in two minutes flat, Justin devours not only my partially eaten half of the sandwich, but the other half, as well.

"I can't believe you can eat at a time like this," I tease.

"Gotta stay strong to keep you safe." He gives me a wink. Not a creepy Dawson-style wink, but a wink that solidifies how close we've become. Justin really has become my friend.

Another warm breeze blows in, and I stare out at the woods, dark and dense.

"It's so dark out there," I say shakily. "How will we even see where we're going?"

"We'll be fine," Justin assures me. "There's a moon out tonight. And just keep reminding yourself you'll see Farren soon. That should keep you going."

It sure does, and it gets me moving, too.

I start to crawl out the window, throwing out over my shoulder, "Yeah, come on. Let's get the hell out of here."

CHAPTER SEVENTEEN

Farren

As night falls, I notice increased activity on the screen. As in, the tracker is on the move.

"Hey," I call over to Rick, tapping the laptop screen as I do, "check this out. There's activity outside the chalet. I think Dawson is up to something."

Rick is at my side in no time. He checks out the laptop screen, and observes, "Hmm, it looks like Dawson left the chalet. That's different. Didn't Justin say he always stays inside?"

"Yeah, he did. Something must be happening."

Leaning back in my desk chair, I watch the GPS light blinking around on the map of the ski lodge. "He's heading to the back of the main building," I say, watching the movement. "Shit, that means he must be heading to the—"

"—helicopter pad," Rick says, completing my sentence.

And with that, I am out of my chair and gathering weapons

like we're heading to a shoot-out. Hell, we may be. But I can't let Essa be taken away. Not again. I thought I could be patient, but I can't.

Grabbing up one of many guns from our arsenal, I say, "I can't sit around and not do anything, Rick. I have to go in."

"Farren, wait." Rick turns to me, concern creasing his brow. "Hold up a sec. Just think about the situation. We need to assess."

I pause. "Okay. What are you thinking?"

"We know the tracker is on Dawson, right?"

"It looks that way, yes."

"That means the kid was successful. Give him a chance to do what he promised. Let him get Essa out of there."

"Uh, I don't know." I begin to load a cartridge in a .45, back in motion. "Justin getting Essa out of there happens only if everything went according to plan. And we don't know what's going on up there."

Rick steps over to me, lowering the gun from my grasp. "We have to trust it's going according to plan, Farren."

He's right. I know he is. This is what partners do—talk each other down from the ledge when one has reached the brink. And I am certainly at the brink.

"Fuck that," I say, at last. "I can't take any more chances with Essa. If Dawson has transportation coming in and she's still in that place, he *will* take her with him."

"We have the tracker on him, Farren. He won't be able to hide."

I bark out a humorless laugh. "You think I'm going to take a chance like that?"

"You said you were willing to," he reminds me. "You agreed to stick to the plan."

"Well, I changed my mind."

Just then the choppy whir of a helicopter flying over the motor lodge disrupts the usual serenity of the area. I don't stop what I'm doing, loading more ammo into more guns.

That is, until Rick grabs the box I'm pulling bullets from. "Listen, Shaw," he says gruffly. "If Dawson has Essa with him right now, he'll be leaving with her in five minutes. It's too late to stop anything." He gestures to the direction of the ski resort. "That copter is up there, landing as we speak."

"Is that supposed to calm me down?" I snap.

"No. But we have to trust the kid got Essa out."

Rick is right, again. Thank God one of us is thinking clearly.

I close my eyes and take a deep breath. Setting the .45 on the desk, I concede, "Okay. I won't go in there guns a-blazing. But I'm not sitting around here waiting for Justin to arrive with Essa. I think we should try and meet up with them."

I see in Rick's dark brown eyes that he's in agreement with me, at least on this point. "I agree," he says. "How do you want to work this, then?"

Resuming the role of lead in what has become our most urgent mission ever, I lay out the details. "We reverse the path Justin is supposed to take with Essa. If he sticks with what I told him, they should be safe. The woods are far too dense for Dawson to go in and nab them, especially in the dark. But Pierson might be a different story. He's younger and stronger. He may have been left behind to go find them."

I know Rick is one step behind me when he asks, "If Dawson is leaving in the copter, why in the hell would he leave Pierson behind to locate Essa and Justin, assuming they did get away?"

I give him a think-about-it look, and he says, "Oh, fuck. If

Pierson is sent after Essa and Justin, it will be because Dawson has ordered their execution."

"Exactly," I say grimly.

Ten minutes later, and armed to the teeth, Rick and I are on the wooded path leading up to the resort.

CHAPTER EIGHTEEN

Essa

JUSTIN and I stumble to the tree line, following an all-out sprint from the chalet. So far, the escape attempt has been a raging success. Let's hope it stays that way.

Out of breath, I place my hands on my knees and bend over. After a beat, I cautiously ask Justin, "No one is following us, right? I'm afraid to look back."

Justin is not as winded as I am, but there are tiny beads of sweat on his forehead. He swipes his head, adjusts his glasses, and scours the area. "No, I think we're safe."

Just as I'm about to relax a smidge a helicopter buzzes overhead, coming dangerously close to the tops of the trees.

"Shit, that's low," I yell over the whirring noise.

Justin and I huddle together behind a tangle of brush to stay out of sight.

"You don't think the pilot saw us, do you?" I worry out loud once he's passed.

"No, I don't think so," Justin says as we watch the copter land behind the main lodge. "We should get out of here, though, like as soon as we can."

"Right," I agree, nodding. "Let's go."

But, for some reason, we don't move, not a muscle. We remain as we are, enthralled by the sight of Dawson's mode of escape landing behind the building, kicking up the wind and rustling the trees.

I lean into Justin and say, "By the time Dawson or Pierson notices we're gone, we should be deep in the forest."

"Yeah, I think so." Justin glances to the dense, and now very dark, woods. "I think we're good. The night should keep us hidden." I nod, and Justin stands. Reaching out his hand to help me up, he says, "Come on, Essa. We need to go."

I take his hand and rise to my feet. "Which way is the trail?" I ask, since I can't discern much in the dark. It's nothing but trees and heavy brush in all directions, and I can't imagine how we're supposed to trudge through the mess. But Justin claims he knows where to go, so I have to trust him.

Leading me to a trailhead, he says, "This is the path we need to take."

"Okay."

With me trailing behind, we start down a narrow trail that's cut into the side of the mountain. The going is slow with all the heavy growth.

"It's so overgrown," I lament as we tromp through knotted brambles and dense brush. "Are you absolutely sure this is the right way?"

"Yes, I'm sure, Essa." Justin throws a quick glance back at me, right as I'm struggling to crawl over a thick-trunked fallen tree.

"Hold up." He doubles back to help me. "Take my hand."

Justin helps me climb over the tree, and then we continue down the trail.

"Everything looks the same," I say at one point. "How do we know we're going in the right direction?"

"I studied the map Farren showed me thoroughly," Justin replies. "We aren't going to get lost."

"I believe you," I tell him, and since my hand is still in his, I give him an encouraging squeeze.

My fate is in Justin's hands, just like the morning at the coffee shop. But this outcome should be quite different. I fully trust him—that's not a problem—but I fear there's still time for Dawson to discover we're gone. I fear he'll send Pierson after us. And what will Pierson do? Kill us, I'm sure.

With that thought brewing in my head, I urge Justin to, "Hurry."

"I'm going as fast as I can," he replies.

There is a lot of brush to push through, and he has to drop my hand in order to break through several wiry branches, as well as stomp a bunch of rangy weeds into submission. I marvel at how adept Justin is at clearing the path so efficiently, but, oddly, as we progress down the hill, instead of going faster, he begins to slow down.

When he comes to a complete stop for no apparent reason, I say, "What's wrong?"

He turns around to face me...and shit.

His face is ghastly pale, tinged blue in the glow of the moonlight streaming through the canopy of leaves provided by the trees.

Placing his hands on his knees, he bends at the waist and gasps for breath. "I don't know what's wrong with me," he says, coughing, "but I suddenly don't feel so good."

I choose not to mention he doesn't look so good, either.

After catching his breath, he leans against a large tree for support. "I felt fine earlier. This is weird."

It is bizarre, and I ask, "When did you start feeling crappy?"

"A few minutes ago my stomach started hurting, but that sort of passed. Now, I just can't seem to breathe right."

I step toward him and place my hand on his cheek, then slide up to his forehead, feeling for a fever. "Oh, my God, Justin, you're burning up."

"Shitty time to come down with the flu," he says, smiling thinly.

His glasses are askew, and I right them for him. And then, gesturing to a fallen tree a few feet away, I suggest, "Let's sit down for a few minutes and rest."

"I would," he begins, "but what if Pierson *is* following us?"

I glance to the forest we've passed through, dark and dense. "There's no way to know for sure," I state, "but I think we're okay."

"All right," he concedes, eyeing the fallen tree like he can't wait to take a rest. "But only for a minute."

"Or two," I say as I help him over to the tree.

One minute of rest become two. Then two minutes of rest becomes three. We end up hanging out on the log longer than intended, but I'm okay with that. Justin clearly needs the rest; he's looking worse than ever.

"It's peaceful here," I say, trying to make conversation not related to Justin feeling so terribly.

"It is," he agrees, his breathing more labored than before.

Suddenly, a large cracking noise breaks the peaceful silence.

Justin and I freeze, staring at each other wide-eyed.

"That sounded like a branch being trampled by a person," I whisper.

"Maybe it was an animal," Justin offers.

"Aah, it must be pretty big then," I say uneasily.

Justin replies, "I think it's time to get out of here."

"Yeah, for sure."

We're on our feet and back on the trail in no time.

When the path opens up a little, we walk more briskly. But, in his weakened state, Justin soon falls behind.

Glancing back to where he is hobbling along, I ask, "Do you want to take another break?"

He says no, so I turn around, set to continue.

And just as I take a step, I slam headlong into a tall and solid male body.

Oh no, Pierson?

CHAPTER NINETEEN

Farren

A BLONDE whirlwind steps around a bend in the trail and slams right into me. "Oomph," she utters as she knocks herself backward. My hands fly to her slender shoulders, steadying her so she doesn't fall.

And then I see her face, beautiful in the moonlight, and just as I remember. Flooded with relief, elation, and most of all, love, I murmur, "Essalin."

I say no more, as words fail me. I can't believe Essa is here, right smack-dab in front of me. And she's actually safe and well.

It takes Essa a few seconds to catch up to where I am, but when she does she breaks down in tears.

Throwing her arms around me, she sobs, "Oh, my God, Farren, Farren, Farren. I can't believe it's really you, that you're really here."

"It's me," I assure her as I hold on to her tightly. "And I'm

145

here."

I don't add what I'm thinking: Now that I have Essa back in my arms, I don't plan to ever let her go. I will not fail her again.

Rick clears his throat, and I'm reminded that Essa and I are not alone. We need to get out of the woods, back to town, and return to the motor lodge. The helicopter is long gone, which is great, but there could still be trouble brewing. Dawson may very well have left Pierson behind, to follow Essa and Justin. Actually, though, I have a feeling Pierson left with Dawson, but I'd rather be safe than sorry.

With all that in mind, I pull away and say to Essa, "We should keep moving."

She takes a step back. "Yes, of course."

I turn to Rick, and he jerks his head to Justin, indicating something is wrong. Justin is off to the side of the trail, bent over, holding his stomach. The kid doesn't look so good.

I walk over to him. "Are you okay to keep walking?" I ask.

Justin came through, he put himself in jeopardy to help Essa, and though I will probably never forgive him completely for aiding Dawson, I'm well on my way to no longer wanting to throttle him.

Hey, it's a start, especially for who I am and what I do.

When Justin lets out a groan, I ask him, "What's wrong exactly?"

He shakes his head. "I don't know, man. I just feel weak and I'm having trouble breathing. I'm also really sick to my stomach."

Essa then tells me, "He was fine back at the chalet. His symptoms started a little while ago."

"While you two were on the trail?" I inquire.

"Yes," she replies. "Right before we ran into you and Rick."

146

"Hmm…" I ponder. "You didn't eat any berries or anything in the woods, did you?"

"Of course not," Essa says.

"What about up at the chalet?"

"The last thing we had was a sandwich. That was right before we left."

I don't like this. I'm worried Justin's illness isn't some random event.

"What are you thinking?" Rick asks me.

"Nothing," I reply. Blowing out a breath, I turn to Justin. "Can you make it the rest of the way?"

He nods weakly. "Yeah, I think so."

Slowly, the four of us resume walking. Essa stays by my side when the path allows it. And when she is beside me, she can't stop holding on to me.

Leaning in at one point, she whispers, "This is surreal. I can't believe Justin and I actually got away. I can't believe I'm here with *you*."

"You are, sweetheart." I drape an arm over her shoulders. "And you did really well. You were very brave to make a run for it."

"I was so scared, though, Farren, *really* scared."

"Hey, you survived and you escaped. And"—I give her a squeeze—"what's important is you're now with me. You'll be safe from here on out."

She frowns and glances back to where Rick and Justin are trailing behind. "What about Justin, though? Something is really wrong with him."

"Yeah, well, we'll get him some help once we're back at the motor lodge. He'll be fine."

Essa is appeased, but, to me, something feels off with this whole situation. It's not like Dawson to give up so easily. I fully expected Pierson to follow, but that clearly isn't happening. He'd be on us by now. It's safe to conclude those two men are long gone.

So, the question remains: why would Dawson let Essa go without a fight? One reason—he is up to something. He has a back-up plan, some clever move he's set in motion. This is all a game to Dawson, not unlike chess.

I imagine him making that move, something I don't yet see. *Check, Mr. Shaw,* I hear him saying with a laugh.

Shit. I damn well better figure out what Dawson has done, before his *check* becomes *checkmate*.

If I don't, we could all be screwed.

CHAPTER TWENTY

Essa

W<small>E</small> emerge from the woods, coming out behind a small, old-fashioned gas station. There's a single sodium lamp attached to the back of the building, lighting our way in a fuzzy jaundiced glow.

"Stay close," Farren says to me as we walk along the edge of the woods, with Justin and Rick still trailing behind us.

It seems no one has followed us, but it's important we remain unseen, particularly by the authorities in town. Farren wants to finish this mess with Dawson without outside involvement. There's no need to worry, though, as we make it to the motor lodge without encountering a single soul.

At the lodge Rick breaks off from our group and heads to the front of the single-level building, where the office is located.

"He's renting two extra rooms," Farren explains. "One for Justin, and one for himself,"

"Oh, okay."

I'm glad this is the new arrangement, since all I want is to be left alone with Farren.

With that thought in mind, I lean in to him. He drapes an arm over my shoulder, and asks, "You holding up okay?"

"Yeah," I reply, nodding. "I'm better now that we're here at the motor lodge."

I press my nose to Farren's chest and breathe him in. "Mmm, you smell so good," I whisper. "I missed you so much."

"I missed you too, sweetheart," he tells me, his voice sad.

There's something in Farren's voice, some sense of uncertainty that I rarely hear when he speaks. He's usually so confident.

Leaning away, I study him. "What's bothering you?" I tentatively ask.

He glances over at Justin, who is looking worse by the minute. He's leaning against the side of the building, head hung low and eyes closed.

"We'll talk about it later," Farren says under his breath.

I know then that something is up. This isn't the flu Justin is dealing with. But before I have a chance to press for more info, Rick rounds the corner, two keys in hand, one of which he presses into Justin's palm.

Justin startles, his eyes flying open. "Oh!" He looks down at the key. "Thanks."

When Justin turns to head to his room, he wavers on his feet, and Rick says, "Hey, you okay there, kid?"

Justin licks his lips, which appear dry and parched, and then he replies. "Yeah, I'm good. I'm sure whatever this is, it will pass. I just need some rest."

When I glance over at Farren, he's eyeing Justin, forehead

creased. It's like he's trying to figure out what is going on here, or he already suspects something. But what could be happening?

"What are you thinking?" I whisper to Farren.

He shakes his head. "Nothing, Essa," is his simple retort.

Hmm, I don't buy it.

When Farren catches Rick's eye there's a silent exchange between the two. And before we disperse to our respective rooms, I hear Farren quietly say to Rick, "Keep an eye on Justin."

"You got it," Rick replies.

Is Farren's comment a reflection of his distrust of Justin, or is he genuinely concerned for some reason? I have every intention of finding out, but when we step in to the room, alone at last, Farren whisks me off my feet and cradles me in his strong arms.

When he sits down with me on the edge of the bed, he leans down to kiss me. And I melt. His lips are soft and gentle as they meet mine. We kiss passionately for a few minutes, with me repositioning myself, sliding my feet to the floor, Farren helping me stand so that I am wedged between his knees.

Reaching out, I touch his jaw. Amazed by him, amazed that we're together, I whisper, "I love you so much. I just need to tell you that, before…anything."

He smiles, the corners of his eyes crinkling in the way I adore. "I love you too, Essa."

Something passes in his emerald gaze that tells me he is troubled, just as I sensed earlier. I consider questioning him to get to the crux of what's bothering him, but before I have an opportunity, he says, "Do you want to talk about what happened up at the ski resort?"

I know then that Farren wants to know if Dawson sexually assaulted me.

"He didn't assault me, Farren," I assure him. "Not in the way you're thinking, anyway. No one up there hurt me in that way."

I watch as the man I love breathes out a genuine sigh of relief. But he tenses when I add, "I did have to kiss Dawson, though."

"What?"

I cringe at the memory of Dawson's leathery, lizard lips on mine. "I didn't want to, trust me. Unfortunately, it was the only way I could get close enough to him to plant the tracker."

"What else happened?" Farren asks, pained.

"He touched my breasts," I whisper.

"That motherfucking—"

Placing a hand over his mouth, I say, "Shh, it's okay. Pierson interrupted him before he could do anything more. And then I escaped. It all worked out."

Farren, still agitated, says, "Justin was supposed to take care of planting the tracker."

I rush to Justin's defense. "He wanted to, Farren, he did. I was the one who pushed to do it."

Shaking his head, he says, "You should have let Justin do it, Essalin."

"Yeah, right," I scoff. "There's no way he ever could have pulled it off. I was the only option." I pause, and add softly, "You have to know that, Farren."

A myriad of emotions pass in his eyes. The rational side of him knows I am right. But the thought of his arch enemy kissing me, touching me, if even for a very good reason, makes Farren livid.

With a humorless chuckle, and confirming my suspicions, he snorts. "Yeah, sure, Essalin, whatever you say."

"Farren, Farren." I reach out and trace the dark stubble

152

growing in along his jaw. "It doesn't matter now. The important thing is that I succeeded."

"I'm still a man, Essa, and a very jealous one at that." He places his hand over mine and lowers it from his face. "I can't help who I am. And I guess I feel like I failed you in some way. For you to have to put yourself in that position…"

He trails off, and I say, "Stop beating yourself up. I'm here, I'm safe."

"Yeah, but, I can't lie, Essa. The idea of that loathsome prick touching you kills me."

I start to open my mouth, longing to ease him in some way. But before I can utter a single word, Farren spins me around, and the next thing I know is I am flat on my back on the bed. He hovers above me, and we both let go, overflowing with emotion. Hurt, pain, regret, it all pours forth.

"Take me," I whisper between clenched teeth as I grab at his shirt, pulling him down to me roughly. "I need it, Farren, I need you."

All of the tension and fear, the adrenaline rushes, the worry, it all culminates to me needing Farren to make me forget. "I don't want gentle." I nip at his bottom lip when he leans down to kiss me. His eyes flash. This is feral, him reclaiming, me submitting. "Fucking make me yours again," I growl.

Flipping me over onto my stomach, Farren rasps in my ear, his tone pure territorial, "You *are* mine, Essa. All mine."

And then he starts to show me just how true those words are.

CHAPTER TWENTY-ONE

Farren

Essa has pushed me to my limits. I was already wound tightly, ready to snap, before I even left the motor lodge. And then finding her, thinking Pierson could be behind us, wanting to take her away again... Not to mention Dawson, kissing her, fucking touching her. Yeah, I'm raw, as close to primitive as a man can get.

Tugging Essa's clothes off roughly, I don't stop until she is naked and vulnerable beneath me.

I undo my jeans.

And Essa, wound as tightly as I am, raises her hips and wiggles her ass. She wants me as much as I want her. "Farren, don't stop," she pleads.

"Wasn't planning on it," I growl, sounding like the alpha I fucking am, especially in this moment.

With my knee, I urge her legs apart. Freeing my erection, I

lower my body to hers and slide my cock along her slick folds. Wet, she is soaking wet, and her juices coat me in seconds. "Fuck, Essa," I rasp, amazed and more turned on that ever.

"Take me," she begs, for the second time tonight. "Remind me of what I've missed."

That's all it takes. With one push, I am sheathed within her. Leaning down, I turn her head so our lips can meet, albeit awkwardly. "Kiss me, sweetheart," I urge. "Kiss me before I fuck the hell out of you."

She giggles. Essa is giddy on lust, and as she angles her face to me, our lips brush, despite the awkward angle.

"You taste so sweet," I murmur against her lips. And when I start to fuck her she feels just as sweet. My thrusts come faster and faster, harder and harder. I can't get deep enough, I want to bury my whole self in her, but the best I can do is lose myself in her, my mind, my soul.

Essa cries out, and I ask, "Should I stop?" I don't want to kill the girl, though death by fucking might not be a bad way to go.

Not to worry, Essa is quite alive. As she writhes beneath me, her hips lifting to accommodate me, she tells me, "Don't you dare stop."

"Good," I grind out, rising to my knees and grabbing her by the hips, lifting her right along with me so our connection isn't lost. "'Cause I don't think I can stop."

I watch as my cock slides in and out of her, and there's no more talking. There are only moans of ecstasy. And then I feel her coming, as do I, emptying into her.

Essa collapses down to the bed on her tummy, while I flip over to my back to lie next to her.

Pulling her to me, I hold her close, and soon we find sleep.

Hours later, we wake together, in the middle of the night. We can't stop touching each other. Nuzzling and kissing, we love again, this time more slowly, less urgently.

"Don't ever leave me again," I say.

"Don't ever let me be taken again," she counters.

"Never."

And then there's more sleep.

A short while later, after a quick run to the bathroom, I return to find Essa sitting in the middle of the bed, the pile of blankets puddling around her.

When she catches me staring, she raises the edge of a blanket to cover herself.

"A little late for modesty," I scoff. Stepping to the edge of the bed, I tug the cover till it falls away.

Essa gives me a sly smile and scoots back on her ass toward the head of the bed, like she's scared of me.

"Ah, feeling playful, are we?"

She nods once, fully aware that I love the chase, the hunt. So, not unlike a stalking lion, I place my knees on the bed and crawl toward her.

When she reaches the headboard and can't go any farther, I raise a brow. "Where do you think you're going to go from there, sweetheart?"

She shrugs, making her tits bounce enticingly. "Guess you got me," she says demurely.

"Looks that way," I agree.

She leans back, and I tell her, "You look delectable," and then I lunge forward, grabbing hold of her.

With my hands on her breasts, she wiggles down until her body is beneath mine. I know what she wants, but I have something else in mind…for now.

When I lower my mouth down her body to her sex, her breathing quickens. "Oh, the anticipation is the best," I whisper, my breaths warming the clit I'm about to take in my mouth.

"Don't tease," she says.

And then she is sucking in a breath, because I don't tease, I do something I do very, very well. Essa tastes delicious, and it seems I can never get enough of her. Her little clit swells beneath my mouth, becoming not so little. I flick and lap lightly with my tongue until she comes hard for me.

Her hands are in my hair, tugging, pulling me up to her. "Farren, please, please."

She wants to fuck again, and who am I to deny her? I move up her body so that we are aligned to make magic happen for the third time tonight, but then I decide to make her want it a little more.

"Kiss me," I demand.

She does, licking the taste of herself from my lips. Hot and wet and fiery, our lips and tongues intermingle. My cock is right where it needs to be. One push and I'll be in, I'll be home.

Shit, I can't hold off a minute longer. "Oh, God," I rasp, thrusting into her, lost in ecstasy

"Not God, Farren." Essa whispers in my ear. "Not God, but Essa."

I chuckle, grinding and thrusting with abandon. My Essa has turned my words from the first time we were together back onto me.

And I love it, just as I love her.

Plunging into her again and again, losing myself in the girl I love, I agree, "Yes, Essa, you and only you. Always."

CHAPTER TWENTY-TWO

Essa

FEEL so much love for Farren, deep in my bones and etched in my soul. I think about this as I lay awake, sleep elusive after so much good sex. Why do orgasms hype up the girl, but leave the guy so sleepy? Another mystery of life, I suppose.

I adjust my head on the pillow next to Farren's so I can watch him sleep in his post-orgasmic glow. Farren Shaw is beautiful, no doubt, post-orgasm or not. Chiseled features, full lips, and dark tousled hair, he's my own Adonis. And I like how he appears so peaceful when he sleeps, so unburdened. In times like these, when the world is shut out, Farren is a different man.

I wonder what it would have been like to know him before he was a soldier. He was always a fighter, though. He was the strength in his family, the glue that held them together after his father left. But was there ever a time Farren was vulnerable?

Maybe now, as I suspect I'm his one vulnerability.

Sighing, I watch him a bit longer. But it's like he knows when eyes are on him. All too soon, he starts to stir. And then he is awake, groggy, but awake.

Rolling to his back, he scrubs a hand up and down his face.

Side-eyeing me, green eyes alight, he asks, "Is everything okay, Essa?"

I smile. "Yes."

Chuckling, he asks, "What were you doing, then? Watching me sleep?"

"Yes, I was."

"Bet that was real exciting," he teases.

"It actually was rather exciting."

He gives me a *yeah, right* look and I amend, "Okay, maybe not so much exciting, but watching you sleep so peacefully made me feel better."

He rolls toward me, placing his hand under his pillow to prop himself up. "Yeah?" he asks. "In what way?"

"Hmm…" I think about it. "I don't know. It's hard to put into words, but watching you like that makes me feel relaxed. I feel happy, happy I'm here with you." I swallow hard, changing gears to something I need to talk about, to get out. "It was scary up at the resort. I wasn't sure I'd make it, you know?"

Farren reaches over and cups my cheek, his thumb grazing over lips swollen from all the kissing throughout the night. "You were brave, Essalin," Farren says. "You made Justin your ally. You stayed calm. You did everything I would have done."

I make a scoffing sound. "Yeah, except you would never have allowed yourself to fall for such a stupid trick in the first place." I sigh. "I know Justin turned out to be an ally, but I was lucky. He could have been a really bad person. I was foolish for trusting him."

Farren doesn't disagree; he's not going to tell me what I did was okay. It wasn't. I accept that. I put my own life in jeopardy, and his.

Sighing, Farren says, "It all worked out okay, babe. That's what matters."

"Thanks to you," I say. "If we hadn't had a place to run to, or you and Rick hadn't met up with us in the woods, who knows what could have happened." My eyes meet his, and I add, "Truthfully, I don't think Dawson would have left without us if he thought we were on our own. He must have known you were close by."

Farren frowns. He removes his hand from my cheek, rolls to his back.

Propping myself up, I ask, "What's wrong? What are you thinking?"

"Something's been bothering me," Farren says.

"What is it?" Worry creeps up my spine as the words leave my mouth.

Farren rubs at dark stubble on his chin and stares up at the ceiling. "It just doesn't make sense."

"What doesn't make sense, Dawson not coming after us?"

"Yes."

Farren is now the exact opposite of how he was when he was asleep. Every burden, every worry, they've all returned to him.

"I don't want you to worry," I whisper as I lean over and kiss the side of his face.

He pulls me on top of him and stares up at me. "I'll always worry when it comes to you. Isn't that what love is, worrying about the other person?"

"That's not all it is," I say.

I peer down at him, but his emotions are unfathomable in the mostly dark room.

"Essa," he begins, "there are things I need to tell you, things about me that you don't know. But you *should* know these things. It's just…" He trails off, and I place my hands on either side of his face.

"Farren," I begin, "I know everything there is to know about you. And there's nothing I would change, not one thing. I accept you for who you are. All of you, every last bit."

Farren doesn't know Dawson gave me a file detailing all of what he sees as his sins, and he now tries to insist, "You don't know everything, Essa. There are things I've done, things I still do—"

I stop him. "I know you killed a man when you and Barnes were away."

His brows shoot up. "How could you know something like that?" Before I can answer, he murmurs, "Fucking Dawson."

"Yes," I confirm. "He told me everything. He has a file on you, and he was hoping the contents, the info on you, would turn me against you."

Farren searches my face, and I see a flash of his only real vulnerability—me. I could have hurt Farren deeply, but I never would have done that, not in a million years.

Leaning down, I shower him in tiny kisses. "I love you, Farren. I always will. I don't care what you did, or what you still do. Dawson told me everything, and it didn't matter…not then and not now. I accept you. I accept everything about you."

He shifts beneath me, and, like that, we are once again joined.

I gasp, and he groans, "Essa, my Essa. I love you so much,

sweetheart."

"I love you, too," I assure him.

And seeing my true acceptance, *feeling* my acceptance in my body's response, Farren whispers to me that I am his peace, his light in a world of dark.

A FEW hours later, I wake with a start. Something is wrong. It is morning, but I am more exhausted than ever.

"I am so tired," I complain as I search for my underwear in the bedding. I find them, and slowly tug pink panties up my legs.

Then, all energy spent, I roll to my side.

Farren stirs next to me. Leaning over me, he kisses my shoulder. "Go back to sleep, Essa. I'm going out for a bit. I'll grab us a late breakfast in my travels."

"Okay," I murmur. And then I am out.

I wake again sometime later, barely able to open my eyes. Plus, I am freezing.

"Brrr…" My teeth chatter uncontrollably. "I must have caught Justin's flu," I say.

"Maybe," Farren replies from across the room.

I try to sit up, but can't. "You're back," I whisper, my head flopping back on the pillow as I state the obvious.

"Yes, sweetheart, I'm back." He sets a cardboard cup of coffee on the desk against the wall, and then he grabs one of his dress shirts from the back of a chair.

"Are you hungry?" he asks. He sits down on the edge of the bed and helps me sit up so I can slide my arms into the soft cotton shirt. When I fumble with the buttons, he helps.

"I'm not hungry at all," I say, sighing. "In fact, my stomach feels kind of funny."

That gets Farren's attention. He feels my head, takes my pulse. "Were you feeling okay yesterday?"

"Great," I tell him.

"Tell me again what you ate last night?"

"Just part of that sandwich Justin brought me for dinner."

Farren exhales loudly. "Essalin, do you know if Dawson or Pierson made that sandwich, or if either man had access to the ingredients?"

I shrug and fall back on the bed. I'm feeling weaker and weaker. So much so now that it's hard to think.

"I don't remember," I say slowly. "I think Justin said they always watched him make my food. In any case, I'm sure they had access to everything."

Before I can ask where this discussion is heading, my eyes close of their own accord. And once again, I fall fast asleep.

At noon—according to the clock next to the bed—I wake again. Without preamble, I blurt out, "Oh, my God." Covering my mouth, I add, "I think I'm going to be sick."

Farren helps me to the bathroom since I'm now as weak as a kitten. Next to the toilet, I crumple to my knees and become violently ill.

"I *must* have gotten the flu from Justin," I say to Farren when I'm done.

He cleans me up with a warm washcloth and helps me to my feet, his only response an uncertain, "Hmm."

As he walks me back to the bed, I see worry in his eyes. I know I'm the cause, but I don't know what he's thinking.

When Farren is tucking me under the covers a tattoo of frantic knocks sound out on the door.

"Farren, you in there?" a male voice calls out, anxious.

"Yeah," Farren calls out. "Hold up a sec."

It's Rick, I recognize his voice. Farren finishes tucking me in, then goes to the door. When Rick steps into the room his eyes go straight to me, like he's assessing something. "Shit," he mumbles.

"What is it?" I ask, searching both men's faces.

Rick replies to Farren, not me. "Justin is still sick, too. And he's taken a turn for the worse. He's *extremely* ill today."

"Is it what I think it is?" Farren asks his friend.

Rick nods curtly. "Yes, I think so. But we'll need to run blood tests to be sure."

"Blood tests," I mumble. "Why?"

The words are no sooner out of my mouth and the worst pain I've ever experienced slices at my insides. If I wasn't lying down already, I'd be falling down.

Another stab of paints hits again, worse than the first, and that is the point where I promptly pass out.

CHAPTER
TWENTY-THREE

Farren

"Dawson fucking poisoned them," I grind out as I am walking into Rick's room. "That's why he let them go so willingly."

"Yes," Rick replies, leaning back against the door to his room after I'm in. "You're right. The blood work results just came in."

Blowing out a breath, I cautiously ask, "What did he poison them with?"

Rick blows out a breath. "Ricin."

I kick at a wastepaper basket out of frustration and crumpled wads of paper fall out when it topples over. "I'm sorry," I say, gesturing to the mess I made. "I'll clean it up, just give me a minute."

Rick shakes his head. "The last thing I'm worried about is the condition of the fucking room. Let housekeeping get it."

Sitting down on the edge of the bed, I quietly say, "Dawson

put that ricin in *Essa's* food. She was his target."

"He didn't count on Justin eating most of it," Rick concurs.

"Yeah, and good thing he did. If either of them had eaten the whole sandwich, they'd be dead."

I rub at my temple. A colossal headache is building.

The next words out of my mouth are a litany of curses so colorful even Rick appears shocked. Okay, maybe not, but still, he definitely knows heads are about to roll. There's only one head I'm thinking of, though—Dawson's. That motherfucker's time is up.

"We need to get something, an antidote, to help Essa," I say once I've calmed down.

"And the kid," Rick reminds me.

"Yeah, right, sure. We'll get some for him, too." Justin is not my top priority. *Sorry, kid.*

"A hospital is out of the question," Rick states, already brainstorming. "There'd be far too many questions."

"They wouldn't have an antidote, anyway," I remind him.

There is no antidote for ricin poisoning. Well, at least not officially. However, I have an alternative. The agency I work for is always coming up with experimental treatments and antidotes for all sorts of poisonings. The possibility of ingesting something deadly is fairly high with the jobs we are sent on.

Quietly, I say to Rick, "There may be another option."

He eyes me curiously. "Oh? And what would that be?"

"It involves an agency I still do some covert work for."

Rick kicks at a piece of crumpled paper near his toe. "I knew you weren't completely out of things, Shaw."

I shrug. "It's not something I can talk about. You know that, Rick."

"Yeah…" He sighs. "…I know. But let me ask you this: is it Black Ops-related?"

I say nothing, and Rick just nods.

After a beat, he says, "So, you're telling me whoever the hell it is you work for has an antidote for ricin poisoning?"

"Yes."

"Will they help, though?" Rick asks, his expression betraying his doubt.

Rubbing the back of my neck, thinking things through, I say, "Yes, I think so."

Rick watches me. He knows something is holding me back from contacting my bosses. Figuring it out, he says, "You don't want them knowing what's been going down with Dawson, do you?"

He's right, of course.

"Dawson is my problem," I state. "I'd prefer not involving the agency."

"You think the powers-that-be will order you to stand down?"

"Possibly," I sigh. "No, I know they will."

Rick mulls my words over, and then says, "Look, I know you want to go after Dawson. I know you want him so badly you can taste it. But if it means saving Essa and Justin, what choice do you have?"

"None." I exhale loudly. "I have no choice at all."

SEVERAL hours later there's a knock on the door to my motor lodge room. I rise from the bed, stretch a little. I've been sitting with Essa for hours, ever since returning from Rick's room. My time's been spent comforting her, keeping her going.

Essa's eyes flutter open when she feels the loss of the warmth from my hands holding hers. "Farren?" she murmurs.

I turn back to her. "Yes, sweetheart?"

"Where are you going?" she whispers weakly.

"Just to the door." Leaning down, I brush blonde locks, damp with sweat, away from her face. I kiss her forehead and feel she's still burning up. "You're going to feel better soon," I promise. "Just hang in there for me."

"Okay, I will…" She trails off, eyes closing.

Reluctantly, I leave Essa. When I open the door there's a man outside whom I've never before seen. I know, though, that he is with the agency. He's standing slightly away from me, his face turned in profile, jacket collar up.

I assess him quickly, as I'm trained to do. He has neatly trimmed gray hair and a bulbous nose. This guy's got a good twenty years on me, but even in his all-dark clothes, and in the waning light, he appears to be as lean and hard as me.

Definitely a Black Ops agent, same as me.

"Are you Farren Shaw?" the mystery man asks as he slowly turns to face me.

"Yes," I reply.

He offers no name in return, which is not a surprise. The antidote he's here to deliver is experimental. It is theirs and I have no right to it. Therefore, I'm to play by whatever rules the agency dictates.

Mystery man looks beyond me to where Essa is tucked under the covers. "Is that her?" he asks.

"Yes."

"Has it been less than twenty-four hours since she's fallen ill?"

"Yes."

His gaze returns to me and he nods curtly. "This treatment I'm about to give you should work then."

I cock a brow. "Should?"

"It *will* work," he corrects.

The man then hands me a vial of liquid and a hypodermic needle.

"I requested two," I remind him as I take the single dosage of antidote.

"I've been ordered to verify there are actually two individuals in need of what I've brought."

This is ridiculous, but this man is only following orders, same as I do when it comes to what the agency wants.

Taking my cell from my pocket, I call Rick. "You got the key to the kid's room?" I ask when he picks up.

He informs me he has a key to Justin's room, so I ask him to meet me outside the room in a few.

Ten minutes later—with the check on Justin made—the mystery man is handing over the second dose of antidote.

And then he's gone.

"Friendly guy," Rick snorts.

I shake my head. "He's just doing his job."

I give Rick the antidote for Justin and return to my room with the dose for Essa. She is worsening and can't even talk now. "I hope this works," I murmur.

It's been less than twenty-four hours, but I'm still worried. This antidote is experimental, after all. There are no guarantees.

Stretching out Essa's arm, I tap for a vein. When I find a good one, I inject her. I whisper, "I love you," to hopefully give her the strength she needs.

And then the waiting game begins.

CHAPTER TWENTY-FOUR

Essa

FEEL so weird, like I am sick with the flu, but not. See, this level of ill is something you not only feel deep in your body, but in your psyche, as well. Additionally, you know the prognosis isn't good when voices around you are kept at a whisper, and you keep hearing words like *poison* and *ricin*. Wicked Dawson, I know now why he so willingly let me and Justin go. No need to re-capture us if we're doomed to die.

I think about the sandwich Justin brought me. I'm remembering more clearly. He did in fact tell me Dawson or Pierson always supervised when he was making my meals. I thought at the time it was because they were worried Justin would slip some kind of weapon in with the food, a weapon I could use against them, but that was never their fear. They were biding their time, making Justin comfortable with their presence, so that when the time came to slip in something to eliminate us,

Justin would never notice.

Of course, since the sandwich was for me, I was obviously the intended target. The sandwich was so large, though, they may have suspected I'd give some to Justin. Two birds, one stone, and all that, right?

A sob escapes me. "I don't want to die," I whimper. I'm too young; I'm only twenty-three.

Farren, who is seated at my bedside, lifts my hand to his lips. "You're going to be fine, Essa." His lips brush against my fevered skin. "I gave you a shot. It will help you."

"You gave me a shot? I don't remember."

"You were out," he informs me.

"What kind of shot was it?"

"An antidote, sweetheart."

"Really? But...how...?"

I am curious as to what I was poisoned with, and how Farren got his hands on a "cure," but I'm far too choked up to continue. I just can't believe Farren found a way to save my life.

I start to cry, and he asks, "What's wrong, baby? You're going to get better, even if it doesn't feel like it yet."

I squeeze his hand and concentrate. He's right—slowly, my strength feels as if it's returning.

"I wasn't thinking the antidote wouldn't work," I try to explain. "It's just... I can't believe you really found a way to save me."

Farren doesn't respond, so I search his face for an answer. His expression is impassive, though, revealing nothing. But, at last, he says, "I love you, Essalin."

His usual sure voice is uneven as he continues. "I will always be willing to go to the ends of the earth to save you."

With Farren, I don't doubt the veracity of his words. And this man literally *could* go to the ends of the earth for me. He'd do anything for me; I know this now more than ever.

We sit quietly for several minutes, lost in our thoughts. My strength continues to return, and Farren waits patiently to see if I truly am all right.

As I become more and more coherent—my mind clearing as the fever reduces—I ask about Justin. "What about Justin?" I say. "Is he getting better, too?"

"Yes," Farren replies, "Rick gave him a dose of the antidote, as well. He seems to be recovering."

Sighing, I close my eyes. "Thank God. I couldn't live with myself if Justin lost his life because of me."

When I open my eyes, Farren is watching me curiously. "You really think highly of him, don't you?"

Frowning, I retort, "I know what you're thinking, Farren. Justin got me into this mess, how could I ever forgive him?" He doesn't disagree, so I continue. "He actually got pulled into this not knowing the whole story. Dawson took advantage of a bad situation Justin was in. His parents had just cut him off and he needed money. He was a victim, too, in that respect."

When Farren asks why his parents cut him off, I explain how they can't accept Justin for who he is. "They've basically disowned him," I add.

Farren's eyes fill with compassion. "That's awful," he says.

"It is," I agree.

Just then Farren's burner phone rings. He picks it up and answers with a curt, "Farren here."

Rick's voice is on the other end, but too muffled for me to make out what is being said. From Farren's unhappy expression, though, I fear it is bad news.

When Farren disconnects and lowers the phone, I sit up. Placing my hand on his forearm, I ask, "What's wrong? What's going on now?"

A muscle ticks in his jaw. "It's Justin," he replies.

"What about him? He's getting better, right? You said Rick gave him the antidote, too."

Farren frowns. "He did, but there's a problem."

"What kind of problem?"

"Justin was getting better, but now he's taken a turn for the worse."

I think about how much more of the tainted sandwich he consumed, and I say, "He took in a lot more of the poison. I couldn't really eat, so I gave him the rest of the sandwich."

"That's why the antidote isn't working." Farren pinches the bridge of his nose, his renewed concern clear. "He needs another dose."

Sighing, I ask, "Yeah, but can you get him another dose?"

Farren shrugs. "Maybe."

Huffing, I reply, "I'm not stupid, Farren. I know you probably got the antidote illegally. I mean, is there even a cure for ricin poising? Like, one that is out there for public consumption?"

He shakes his head. "No, Essa, there is not."

"So, where did the antidote come from?" I press.

"From a source I can't divulge."

"The agency you work for?"

"Yes."

"You can't give me a name?"

"No."

"Well, can you at least call and get more?"

Chuckling humorlessly, Farren says, "It doesn't work that way, Essalin. Not to mention, I'm trying to stay under the radar. If the agency learns of my plans to go after Dawson, I will probably be ordered to stand down."

Suddenly, I know what I need to do. It's my turn to put myself out there and on the line for Farren. This is my one chance to help, and to show Farren I truly believe in him, and that I back him in every conceivable way.

Resolved, I whisper, "I'll do it, Farren."

That's right—I'm willing to be the same as him.

"You'll do what?" he asks.

"If it comes down to it," I go on. "If you are ordered not to go after Dawson, I will be the one to take him out."

Farren barks out a laugh, and then looks at me like I'm crazy when I'm not laughing, too.

"Essalin, you can't be serious," he says.

"I am totally serious," I assure him.

He exhales loudly. "This isn't something to be taken lightly."

"I'm not taking anything lightly," I maintain.

Shaking his head, he says, "Even if I agree to your crazy idea, you've not been trained on the right kinds of weapons."

"I did fine with the gun out in the desert," I remind him.

"This would be far different."

I know Farren doesn't want me to become what he is, but some part of him must see that after all I've been through, I am halfway there.

"My mind is made up," I tell him. "I want to do it."

"Essa..."

"I'll be well soon," I continue, "We can go after Dawson then. We'll travel to wherever the tracker leads us. It will be just the same as if you were on your own, except I'll be the one pulling the trigger."

Farren cups my cheek. "This isn't you, Essa," he whispers.

He's so wrong. "This *is* me," I insist vehemently. "I am not so very different from you."

Farren stares into my eyes, gauging my commitment. I know he sees I'm serious when he relents, a little. "It's not just about learning to use the right weapon, Essa. It's a mindset, as well."

Placing my hand over his, I hold his gaze. "Dawson poisoned me, Farren. And when he abducted me, he tried to turn me against you. Hell, I had to kiss the man, let him grope me." Quietly, I add, "And he would have made me do *much* more, Farren, if I hadn't escaped."

Farren, ever the alpha, lets out a feral growl. "Essa, stop it."

"No." I shake my head. "You talk about having the right mindset, but what you don't realize is I'm already there. I have been for a while. I've been in survival mode since I turned in that alley and saw I'd made a huge miscalculation."

"If I say okay," he says, hedging, "what would you need for me to do to get you ready?"

"I need you to teach me to be like you, Farren." I hold his gaze intently. "And then I need you to commit to letting me be the one to end this. Agree to let me kill Dawson."

CHAPTER TWENTY-FIVE

Farren

Is Essa fucking nuts? Has the poison messed with her brain? Part of me wants to believe these things so I can pass off her demands as foolish talk. However, in my heart of hearts, I know the truth—Essalin Brant's mind is working just fine. She is what she's always been—a woman ready for the next adventure.

Well, she sure as fuck found adventure with me, adventure on top of adventure, in fact, some good, some bad. Essa wanted to live and take chances. She got that…and more. My life teeters on the edge of a razor, and one thing is certain—when you're on the brink, life is never dull. You live every minute, you *feel* every minute. All because you never know if that minute may be your last.

But, still, over the next few days, I find myself checking again and again with Essa to make sure this is what she really wants to do.

"You sure you want to do this?" I ask her a week after the subject of her being the one to kill Dawson was first brought up.

We're no longer in upstate New York. We've moved down to DC, for now. We are ensconced on the top floor of a luxury hotel in the downtown area. And what I feared might happen when I contacted my agency for more of the ricin antidote indeed occurred. I was given more antidote, and Justin got better, but I was also ordered to stand down, to leave Dawson be.

After I put in the request for a second dose, that ball was rolling. Dose number two was delivered by the same no-name mystery man. He had a message for me this time, though, an order to abandon my quest for justice. I was told the agency doesn't care if Dawson is killed; they just don't want me to be the one to do it. They're concerned my identity could be revealed if something goes awry.

It's not worth jeopardizing our best sniper, the mystery man informed me.

So here I am with Essa in DC, training her to be me. Fucked up, right?

Nonetheless, we are at a shooting range at FBI headquarters. Vincent was kind enough to set up private time for Essa to practice at their range. He also shut down all closed-circuit TVs so we'd have complete privacy.

Me, I've brought along a few of the best sniper rifles in existence. This particular FBI shooting range was the only viable option. I couldn't exactly show up with Essa to the place I normally shoot. That location, tucked away in Arlington, doesn't exist. Same as I don't exist as an agent of Black Ops.

Essa aims at a target, adjusts her sights. "Yes, I'm sure, Farren," she replies, answering my earlier question.

She then proceeds to blow the hell out of her target.

"Shit," I murmur. "You really are a natural at this."

Hell, I don't know if I should find my girlfriend's accuracy with a gun scary or appealing. I lean toward appealing, since Essa with a gun in her hands never fails to turn me on.

Setting the rifle down, she takes off her protective eye gear and removes the plugs from her ears.

"What is it?" she coyly asks when she sees the suggestive glint in my eyes.

I sidle up behind her and wrap my arms around her. "Do you have any idea of how amazingly sexy you look right now?"

She leans back into me, no doubt feeling how aroused I am already.

Yep, she feels it. I'm certain when she breathes out a wispy, "Oh, *oh*..."

We are completely alone, so I have no qualms about feeling her up a little. Undoing the buttons on her thin blouse, I slide my hand over her soft skin and slip my fingers under her bra. Her nipples feel hotter than the rest of her as they pebble beneath my pliant touch.

When I stop, she begs, "Don't, Farren. Keep going."

I turn her to me, giving her a reassuring smile that I have no intention of stopping, and two minutes later Essa's blouse is completely undone and halfway off. Her front-closure bra has been unclasped, leaving her breasts exposed to me. I've also ensured her cute little slacks and even cuter lacy thong are down around her knees.

Unzipping my jeans, I slide the denim material down my hips, along with my boxer briefs. And then I bend Essa over a nearby table covered in ammo and guns. Fuck, her ass is creamy and inviting, and I waste no time entering her from behind.

She gasps, "Yes, yes," over and over as bullets fall to the floor in a clatter. I respond by thrusting into her with abandon.

I'm going at it at a good pace, but Essa urges, "Faster, Farren, do it harder."

Chuckling, I indulge her. She loves the illicit nature of what we're doing as much as I do. That's why she wants it rough. Indulging her, I grab her hips and pump into her vigorously. Soon, we are coming undone together.

When Essa collapses forward onto the table, I lean over her satiated body and brush her moist hair away from her neck. Her skin is slightly damp, so when I kiss her skin I taste salt. "Delicious," I murmur.

Essa's breathing quickens. "That feels so good, Farren," she groans. "Just kissing me like that, I love it."

I'm ready to flip her over and dive down between her thighs so I can lick and kiss her in an even more satisfying manner, but then she reminds me we have places to go.

"If you don't stop doing that," she whispers, "we'll never get out of here."

I nip at her skin. "Do you want to get out of here?"

She groans. "Not really. But if we don't leave soon the visiting hours at the hospital are going to end."

Ah, Essa wants to see Justin. And she is correct about the visiting hours. I know it's important to her to check in on her friend, so I help her up, albeit reluctantly, and aid her in straightening her clothes.

Justin is in DC, as well, He's at a nearby hospital. With the help of Vincent we were able to secure a private room for him under an assumed identity. He received the second antidote before we left the Adirondacks, but he was still pretty bad off. The kid will be fine in the long run, but for the time being he needs IV fluids and electrolytes to get him back on track. The ricin really fucked with his system, much more so than with Essa.

An hour after we leave the shooting range, we are standing at Justin's bedside.

"You look so much better," Essa says to him as she adjusts the covers on his narrow hospital bed.

"I feel a lot better, too," Justin replies.

She puts her hand on his and tells him, "I'm so glad you're going to be okay."

"Thanks to Farren," Justin says to me with a grateful nod.

"Glad you're feeling better," I say sincerely. "Things were a little touch and go there for a while."

"I know," he says. "The doctors and nurses told me the same. I'm just glad I don't remember much, just a lot of crazy dreams."

"I bet," Essa says.

"Hey," I interject, "I hear you're getting discharged soon."

"Yeah," Justin replies. "They tell me I'll be out of here in another day or two." He gives Essa a knowing look and adds, "Of course, I wouldn't mind hanging around just a little bit longer."

I'm utterly confused, until Essa says, "Ohh, you and Doctor Hottie are hitting it off, yeah?"

Seems Justin has a crush on his doctor and has obviously confided this to Essa.

"You should ask him out," Essa whispers.

A second later, as if on cue, a young blond guy who looks like a California beach bum, if not for the white lab coat, saunters in. "How's my favorite patient feeling today?" beach bum-doctor says to Justin with a smile.

Essa and I step back to give the doctor access to Justin's bed, and as we do, I murmur, "Looks like the feeling is mutual."

She excitedly, but quietly, replies, "I know, right? It's so awesome. Justin deserves some happiness after all he's been through."

"Yeah, he does," I agree, realizing then that I have fully forgiven Justin. He's a good guy who got caught up in a bad man's web. At least something good has come out of it for the kid, as Justin and the doctor can't keep their eyes off each other.

"We should go," Essa whispers to me.

I nod, and she sends a good-bye wave to Justin. She makes a motion that he should text her later, which makes him smile.

"Love is in the air," she says when we are outside the room.

"Yeah, it seems it is," I agree.

It's true, and not just for Justin and the young doctor. Rick is back in New York City with Haven, keeping her safe. And I am here with Essa, a woman I'd do anything for.

And that's when it hits me. I don't want Essa to be the one to shoot Dawson. No, I can't ask that of her. Fuck the agency. When it comes time to take out Dawson, Essa can aim the rifle all she wants, but *I* will be the one to pull the trigger.

CHAPTER TWENTY-SIX

Essa

THE tracker is still on Dawson, which is good news. He must take that damn suit jacket everywhere. Hopefully, he won't take it to the dry cleaners—or, God forbid, discover the tracker—before we get to the prick.

When I ask Farren he informs me Dawson is back out west. He's in Arizona this time, not New Mexico. Unfortunately, he is moving around too much for us to fly out and set up.

"How much longer do we have to wait?" I ask one night.

We're in our very nice, very luxurious hotel room, seated at a bank of computers set up in front of floor-to-ceiling windows overlooking DC. The view is stunning, but I can't keep my eyes off the screens that track Dawson's movements.

Farren exhales and leans back in his chair. He swivels toward where I am perched on the edge of the desk. "Not much longer now, Essa," he says, stretching, the hem of his dress shirt edging up, revealing his taut abs. "It looks like Dawson is finally staying put."

I pry my eyes from Farren's hot body, which isn't easy, to focus on the blinking light.

Dawson's current location appears to be outside of Tucson, and I wonder aloud, "What's out there in the middle of the desert?"

"Probably another house of his," Farren replies. "I'll have more intelligence on the property later tonight."

I glance out the window, the setting sun tinting all the buildings in a bruised purple. "It'll be dark soon," I say softly. "We should think about eating dinner."

Time these days is filled with target practice and learning how to think like a sniper would. Farren is training me how to get my mind right about what I need to do—kill Dawson. I hope he's not just appeasing me. I worry, though, that Farren will go against agency orders.

I can't let that happen.

Farren places his hand on my knee. He makes circles on the bare skin exposed below the hem of the light burgundy summery dress I'm wearing.

Raising a brow, he queries, "So, do you want to go out to dinner,"—his hand moves up an inch—"or order in some room service."

It seems I crave Farren's touch more than ever these days, so it's an easy decision to make. "Let's order in."

It takes us another hour to get around to thinking about placing a room service order, as Farren has other things in mind to fill our time before we eat.

Finally, though, with Egyptian cotton sheets wrapped around

my bare body, I sit cross-legged in the middle of our huge bed, perusing the room service menu.

"What about burgers and fries?" I call out to Farren.

He laughs as he comes to stand in the doorway of the en-suite bathroom. A towel hangs low on his waist, his skin damp from showering, and all his enticing muscles accentuated.

Just as I am seriously considering delaying dinner for another hour, Farren waylays that plan when he says, "I'm starving, Essalin. I think I might need something more substantial than a burger."

I stretch languorously, letting the sheet fall away. I'm such a tease.

"Guess we did engage in some activities that would work up a man's appetite…" I trail off, glancing away demurely. I love to flirt with this man.

Farren strides over to the bed and grabs my ankles. He's already growing hard beneath the towel. As he drags my body to him, I yelp, and then pretend to try to get away.

"Playing coy, sweetheart?" he asks, releasing me.

In my most innocent voice, I stop resisting. I turn to him and say, "No, not at all."

I lie back on the bed, knees up. Farren watches as I open my knees just a little bit, giving him a glimpse of what I so much want to give him.

His breathing quickens, his hard chest rising and falling in tandem. "Essalin," he growls. "You are a very, very naughty girl."

I allow my legs to fall open completely, and say, "Maybe you should punish me, then."

One does not play games with Farren Shaw. He will always,

always win. And win he does when he drops the towel from his waist and kneels on the bed, his muscular body caging me in. I am at his mercy.

"Say it again," he rasps.

All too willing to give in to him, I groan, "Punish me. Please."

A second later my arms are pinned above my head. Another few seconds blur by, and Farren is pressing down on me. "A-a-a-h," I groan, throwing my head back when he enters me.

Farren's uses his free hand to lift one of my legs higher. "How deep can you take it, Essa?"

My response is a moan. Truth is I can't find my voice to answer. I am too caught up in the heady feeling of Farren restraining me, filling me. He reminds me with every measured thrust that I am his. He made me this way when he awakened the woman within me, the one I was always holding back. But with Farren I embrace who I've become.

He pulls out almost all the way and goes still, teasing me. "Tell me you love me, Essalin."

"I love you," I whisper.

"Say it again."

I get another inch, nothing more.

"I love you," I say a little louder.

Farren stills again.

I am at the brink, and I need him to move. "Please," I beg. "Please, Farren,"—I roll my hips—"I love you. I love you. You know I do."

He falls onto me, his hard body crushed to mine. "I know you do, sweetheart. I know you do."

And then he moves—finally—and it's at a nice and steady

pace that feels like an expression of his love. No more games for tonight, just raw feelings.

Needless to say, it is close to midnight by the time we finally eat dinner.

CHAPTER TWENTY-SEVEN

Farren

THE next morning, after I receive more intelligence on Dawson's precise location, I let Essa know it is finally time to leave DC.

"He's definitely in Tucson?" she asks, double-checking.

"Yes, just outside of, same location as before."

Essa appears nervous as hell, so I remind her, "You don't have to do anything you don't want to. We'll fly out to Arizona together, and we'll set up at a location near the house Dawson is staying in. But when it comes down to taking him out, I'll pull the trigger, Essa."

"Yeah, but… You're under orders not to shoot Dawson."

"Just let me worry about that. You're more important to me than any fucking orders, no matter who issued them."

Essa turns away and resumes packing. I know she wants to be strong, but my mind is made up. There is no more discussion, and several hours later we are landing at a regional airport near Tucson.

On the way to the car I arranged with a buddy—I needed transportation waiting and ready—I make peace with my final decision. And that decision is: I am definitely going to be the one to kill Dawson.

Hell with the fallout.

Essa was unusually quiet on the flight, meaning this is becoming too much for her. She is not mentally built like me, despite all her arguments to the contrary.

So things are set in my mind. But then I receive a reminder message from headquarters to not do anything stupid.

"It's like they can read my goddamn mind," I mutter as I read the text on my burner phone, and then promptly delete it.

Essa is at the passenger door of the nondescript car my buddy has selected for us. A dry, hot wind blows dust and sand across the tiny airport parking lot.

With her hand on the door handle, but unmoving, Essa asks, "What is it, Farren? What's wrong?"

"Nothing." I blow out a breath. When she looks over at me, I open the driver's door and wave her off. "We'll talk about it later. Right now we need to get going."

"Okay."

Like two true partners, we slip into the white sedan at the same time. I'm happy with the vehicle choice. This car will fit in anywhere, even though it is far but ordinary. The trunk happens to contain two state-of-the-art sniper rifles, M24s. There's also surveillance equipment, transmitters, and much more stashed in the car. My associate, a guy who works the southwest, "prepped" the car for me. He'll be providing look-out, as well, when Essa and I set up to take out Dawson.

I do have to smile, though, when Essa starts checking under the dash and in the spaces between the seats. "What are you searching for?" I ask, amused.

"Listening devices, explosives, that sort of thing. You can't be too careful, right?"

I place my hand on hers, halting her search through the middle console. "It's clean," I assure her.

With a tilt of her head, she assesses me. "You had someone leave this car here for us, didn't you?"

"Yes."

"Aha!" She smacks my hand playfully. "So, I'm wasting my time checking it over."

With my foot on the brake, but before I hit the Start ignition button, I hold her gaze. "Absolutely not, Essalin," I say seriously. "It's always better to be safe than sorry."

"Does this associate have a name, by chance?" she asks.

Essa knows the man who delivered the car wasn't Rick, since he's in New York with Haven.

"I can't talk about him, Essa," I say quietly.

When I sigh, she says, "Is he with the agency you work for?"

I nod. "Yes, and it's safer for you if you don't know his name."

Essa stares straight ahead, not giving away anything, so I ask, "You sure you're okay with this? 'Cause this is how shit goes down in my world. We don't get names all the time, and we *never* know all the details of the mission we're on."

Essa is smart, though, she knows there's more to it than that. "This guy is helping you without the agency knowing," she states.

I scrub my hand down my face. It's hot in the car, even with the air now running. "Yeah," I admit. "The agency doesn't know he's helping me."

"Because you're not supposed to be here," she whispers. "The orders to stay away from Dawson still stand."

"Yes," I sigh, "they sure do."

Essa places her hand on my knee. "If that's the case, then I won't allow you to get in trouble. Your agency is clearly serious about this. I'll pull the trigger, Farren. I can do it, I swear I can."

"I don't know, Essa."

She is insistent, however. "Farren, seriously, I thought about it on the whole flight here. I know I look shaky, but truthfully, I am ready. I want to do it...for us, for you."

It's pretty hard to find the right words to respond to a girl who is willing to kill for you, all in order to save your hide.

So, without replying, I just hit the gas and go.

CHAPTER TWENTY-EIGHT

Essa

FARREN and I set up on a high bluff above the house Dawson is staying in.

And then we wait.

Peering down at the modest adobe building, it appears to be the lone structure settled in a bowl of sand, nothing but mountains all around. Not that my view is all that great. The hour is late and it's getting dark out in the middle of nowhere. Soon, the only light will be from the moon and the millions of stars peppering the night sky.

"I feel like we might be the only two people left in the universe," I say to Farren, peering up wistfully at the stars. "That is," I qualify, "if we were here for any other purpose."

"Other than to kill Dawson," Farren says, putting to words what I was trying to say.

"Yes, other than that."

Farren is attaching a scope to one of the sniper rifles—mine—but he stops so he can look over at me and assess my current state of mind. He worries about me, my commitment to do this, but I am fine. I think...

Frowning, Farren asks, "Are you sure about this, Essa?"

Blowing out a breath, I reach for the rifle. "Yes," I state, "I can do it, and I'm as ready as I'll ever be."

Farren nods. "Okay, then, let's take our positions."

There is an outcropping of boulders at the edge of the bluff, affording us a clear view of the front of Dawson's hideout. Farren sets up our rifles, and we take our spots—side-by-side, on our stomachs.

Peering through the scope I realize how much smaller this place is compared to the estate where Farren and I met with Dawson back in May. Farren informed me earlier that this is a safe house for Dawson, a temporary residence that no one—except for us, and only thanks to the GPS tracker—knows about.

After surveilling the area for the next several minutes, Farren determines there is only one guard on the premises.

"That looks like Pierson," I tell Farren when I find the guard in my sights.

Farren, peering through the scope of his own rifle, agrees, "Yeah, I think so, too."

"What should we do about him?" I ask.

"I brought a tranquilizer pistol," Farren says. "I'll incapacitate him in a minute."

"All right." My heart pounds, this is real and very fucking scary.

Farren, calm as can be, says, "When Pierson goes down, Dawson may suspect something is up. I wouldn't be surprised if

192

he's watching from one of the windows. He's a paranoid fucker like that."

I nod, my voice lost momentarily.

Farren reaches for the tranquilizer pistol—which I originally thought was just an extra gun tucked in the back of his waistband—and takes a good look at me. My hands are shaking, and I'm sure my face is pale.

"Essa…" He places his hand on my shoulder, sighs.

"I'm fine," I bite out.

He shakes his head, doubtful. "You don't look fine, babe."

Looking up at him, I tell him what I'm thinking. "Okay, I'm scared to death, Farren. But I'm ready. I'll do whatever I have to do. I may be nervous, but I'm not backing out."

He squeezes my shoulder once, and then resumes his position. "Things could happen fast," he tells me. "Just follow my lead."

"Uh-huh."

With sweaty palms, I grasp the trigger and lower my gaze to the scope on the rifle. I know Farren's associate, who is somewhere nearby, is ready to whisk us out of the desert when the time comes. I'm sure Farren also ordered him to hold any guards we come across for questioning later, which, in this case, would be Pierson.

Farren suspects Dawson's whole organization will topple once he's gone. That means no more human trafficking, at least not from that particular source. *Hey, it's a start*, I reason. And thinking of all the girls who will be spared, I muster the courage I need. I'm ready to do whatever I need to do tonight, including shooting Dawson.

Farren aims the tranquilizer pistol and fires. Pierson goes down on the first shot.

"He'll be out for a while," he assures me. "My associate will pick him up later."

"After he gets us out of here, right?" I don't care to stick around any longer than I have to once the deed is done.

"Yes, that's the plan."

We both fall silent, waiting and watching for Dawson to emerge from the house. It feels like an hour passes, but it's actually only a few minutes before Dawson emerges from the front door.

He pauses at the stoop, looks around. He then sees Pierson. Quickly, his gaze darts left and right. When he assumes he's safe he hurries over to where Pierson's body lies prone in the barren front yard.

Dawson freezes, though, before he reaches him. He must sense something is up. Slowly, he takes a pistol from beneath his suit jacket.

Spinning around, he assesses his surroundings. I swear I see him smiling when he glances up to the top of the bluff.

"Now, Essa," Farren commands.

My finger is on the trigger, and I have Dawson in the crosshairs.

But, I…can't…move.

"Farren," I whisper, "I don't know if I can do it."

He shimmies over to me, his fingers covering mine in a firm grip. "Just pull the trigger," he whispers. "Here"—his fingers flex—"I'll help you."

I nod once.

"Is he still in the crosshairs, Essa?"

"Yes."

Farren's fingers tighten over mine, and together we fire the shot that drops Dawson to the ground.

"He's down," I whisper.

Farren aims and shoots once more, his shot piercing Dawson's chest. "Now, we can be sure he's dead," Farren whispers.

And then everything catches up to me, and I am sobbing, sobbing uncontrollably as Farren enfolds me in his arms.

"Essa, Essa." He kisses my cheek, his lips brushing away my tears. "It's okay, sweetheart. It's over. It's done. And you did great."

"I panicked." I start to cry harder. "You had to do it. You fired the fatal shot. I feel like I failed you."

"Hey, hey, look at me, Essa." He brushes hair from my face, and I tentatively glance up at him. "You didn't fail, sweetheart," he tells me. "Dawson is gone."

"Are we sure he's dead?"

I look down to where Dawson is lying on the ground. Farren's mysterious associate is checking over the body. Farren follows my gaze, and the mystery man gives him a thumbs-up.

"He's dead, Essa," Farren says quietly.

"I should have been able to do it alone," I bite out, angry at myself.

Farren cups my cheek and peers into my eyes, calming me. There's peace to be found in his soothing emerald gaze.

My breathing steadies, and Farren whispers, "When it comes down to it, Essa, we did this the way we do things best."

"And how is that?"

"Together."

I smile. "Yes, together."

Farren leans down and kisses me, just a light brush of his lips, and I know he is right.

CHAPTER TWENTY-NINE

Farren

SOMETIMES things really do work out the way they are meant to be. However, there was once a time I believed quite the opposite. I used to think it was a rare event for things to go smoothly, go right. But Essa has made me see my life differently and, more importantly, more clearly.

These days I find myself believing in things like soul mates, destiny, and true love. The one thing of which there is no doubt is that I love Essalin Brant, truly. Fuck, do I love that girl.

And I know we'll spend forever together. Together, yeah, the way we took care of things in Arizona.

Speaking of which, the fallout from Dawson's demise has, surprisingly, been minimal. Sure, the agency suspects I was involved somehow. After all, I was in the state of Arizona when Dawson went "missing."

Luckily for me, they can't prove my involvement. And that

leaves me off the hook.

How is that possible?

Well, first, there is no body. My associate—who continues to remain anonymous to everyone but me—took care of any and all evidence, including Dawson's body. He cleaned up the blood, disposed of all our rifles, and got me and Essa the hell out of Tucson in record time.

All that was left was an empty house out in the desert.

Pierson was taken in before he woke up. I questioned him at an undisclosed location the next day. Then, he was turned over to Vincent's people and flown to FBI headquarters in DC.

I don't know where Pierson will end up. Prison, most likely. He'll receive a reduced sentence, though, for the helpful information he's thus far provided. We've been using that info—along with the FBI—to dismantle Dawson's human trafficking operation. With Dawson out of the picture, cracks in the business have turned to fissures. We keep pushing, and things keep toppling. I suspect it will all be over soon. For that, I am thankful.

Haven is ecstatic with the new developments, as would be expected. She's turned her terrible experience into a commitment to help others. She's involved with helping victims of sexual slavery, and she's so committed that she's staying on in New York City. She's already put in a transfer to Columbia, so it looks like she and Essa will spend their senior year of college together, after all.

On the relationship front, Rick and Haven are going strong. He found an apartment nearby, and already he and Haven are dividing their time between my place and his. I don't know where things with them will end up, but I suspect marriage is a possibility.

Rick as my brother-in-law…yeah, I can live with that.

I smile, as I am pretty damn happy about a lot of things these days. One, I have all the time in the world to hang out with—and dote on—Essa. That should be the case until duty once again calls. And that will happen, of course, as I am as actively involved as ever with the same doesn't-really-exist Black Ops agency as I was with before.

That's okay, though. I've accepted my duty and my obligation, and so has Essa.

Seated out on the balcony of my apartment, high above Central Park, I lift a bottle of beer to my lips and take a long pull. The sun is reflecting off the tall buildings, beyond the greenery of the park, as it sets in the west, turning the steel facades to a golden hue.

"I love this fucking view," I murmur.

The sliding door opens behind me, and I twist in my chair to watch Essa step out onto the balcony.

"Hey, there you are," she says. "I was looking all over for you." She pulls up a chair and sits down next to me. With her hand going to my knee, she adds, "I should have known you'd be out here."

I smile. Essa knows where I go to relax and reflect.

I place my hand over hers. "I'm glad you found me, sweetheart."

I mean so much more than her finding me out here on the balcony, and when our eyes meet, she knows it, too.

"I love you," she mouths.

Suddenly, I have a burning desire to take her inside and have her all over the apartment. Not that we haven't done that a dozen times before, but it's always a good time.

Clearing my throat, I ask, "Are Haven and Rick around?"

Essa hears the rawness in my tone, the want and longing I feel, the need to be with her all the time. Slyly, she replies, "They went over to his place."

I raise a brow. "Oh, they did, did they?"

Essa can't stop smiling at me, and that is just fine for me. I can't quit smiling at her, either.

I stand, and, scooping her up in my arms, carry her into the apartment. Essa kisses my neck and rakes her hands through my hair. She's as anxious as I am to touch…and hold…and just love one another.

And that's what it comes down to. In all this turmoil, and through whatever detours and circumstances that have come our way, love has always won, and it will continue to prevail.

EPILOGUE

Essa

MARCH in New York, seven months following the ordeal with Dawson, and life is good.

This year's winter held on tightly, but there's now a touch of spring in the air, a renewal of life that can't be denied.

Still, gathering one last gasp, snow falls the first day of Spring Break.

"I am so glad we're leaving for the beach tomorrow," Haven moans.

"You're not kidding," I agree as I fold a pair of denim shorts and toss them in her suitcase.

I'm in her bedroom at Farren's apartment, helping her pack. We're leaving for the Dominican Republic tomorrow, a trip Farren planned for the four of us a few weeks ago. Rick should be here assisting Haven, the procrastinator, but he managed to run out with Farren on some guy-oriented errand.

Helping Haven pack has thus been passed off to me. Not that I mind, it gives me time to talk with my best friend. It seems we're always so busy with our guys these days that we rarely have time alone.

Moving Haven's suitcase aside, I scoot back on the bed. "I can't wait to be on the beach, lounging in the sun, and drinking a daiquiri," I proclaim.

"Yeah, me too," Haven replies distractedly from in front of her closet. Her hand is on her hip, surveying, as she asks, "How many dresses are you taking with you, Essa?" She starts flipping through her clothes, hangers clattering. "I'm thinking one for each night. We'll be going out a lot, right?"

I shrug, but she can't see me with her back turned.

When she comes over and dumps a bunch of dresses into her suitcase, I remind her, "We're only staying for five days, Hav."

Walking back to the closet, she says, "Hey, I'm the fancy one here. You may like all your casual attire, but I'm a dressy kind of girl."

She's got me there.

"Here, catch," she says, tossing a skirt at my head. "You can borrow that one. It's short. My brother will like it."

I catch the skirt, and when our eyes meet we start laughing. It truly does feel like old times.

Content and happy, I start folding clothes that didn't make it into the suitcase.

"Thank you for helping me, Essa," Haven says softly.

"Anytime," I reply, smiling.

She turns from the closet to a dresser and begins rummaging through the drawers. I have to say Haven looks good. She's gained back some much-needed weight. Rick takes her out to dinner all the time, usually for big pasta meals, so I'm not surprised. I suspect returning her to a normal weight has always been his goal. He really does love Haven, and he's definitely great for her.

And I'm pleased to report the two of them are now a couple *in every way.*

Still, becoming physical with Rick was a big step for Haven. He was patient and understanding, and when it happened, Haven later told me she was more than ready. She also said she finally knew what real love felt like.

I smile to myself at the notion that everyone who is important in my life is happy and in love, including Justin, with whom I've remained in contact. Justin and the blond doctor are dating. They're going really strong, and I'm glad since Justin's family is still refusing to talk to him. *Maybe in time…*

Sighing, I push all sad thoughts from my head.

I think of Farren and my life with him. Things couldn't be better. It seems we grow closer with every day that passes. And we are learning more and more how to live with one another. One thing is we never sweat the small stuff. Not after what we've been through. And, sure, I worry every time Farren has to "go away" for the agency. But what it all comes down to is this: I believe in him.

And that statement applies to our relationship, this life we're building, in several ways.

I believe the inevitable detour that brought Farren Shaw into my life was part of our destinies. The inevitable circumstances that landed me in Dawson's clutches were fate's way of bringing out all the secrets Farren was afraid to tell me. He needed my acceptance to move to the next level with me, and I can safely say Farren's trust in me now mirrors my own trust in him—both, indestructible.

That's a damn good foundation, trust and love. And if we don't allow those things to falter, I have a feeling Farren and I will remain together, forever.

THE END

Acknowledgements

Thank you to all the readers, the people who take time to review, the bloggers who support my books and help me get the word out there, my incomparable street team, and, of course, my wonderful family and friends! I couldn't do what I love to do without you and your unwavering support. On the technical side of things, much gratitude to Becky and the editing team at Hot Tree Editing, Ari at Cover It! Designs, and the formatting team at E.M. Tippetts. You all rock!

About the Author

S.R. Grey is an Amazon Top 100 and Barnes & Noble Top #1 Bestselling author. She is the author of the popular Judge Me Not series, the Inevitability duology, A Harbour Falls Mystery trilogy, and the new series of Laid Bare novellas. Ms. Grey's works have appeared on Amazon Bestseller lists, including Top 100 multiple times, as well as Barnes & Noble, #1 in Bestselling Nook books.

Ms. Grey resides in Pennsylvania. When not writing, Ms. Grey can be found reading, traveling, running, or cheering for her hometown sports teams.

Author Website:
srgrey.com

S.R. Grey Facebook:
www.facebook.com/pages/SR-Grey/361159217278943

Sign up for S.R. Grey's exclusive-content newsletter and never miss an update, cover reveal, or release:
mad.ly/signups/106801/join

Follow S.R. Grey on Twitter:
twitter.com/AuthorSRGrey

Find blog posts on the S.R. Grey Goodreads Author page:
www.goodreads.com/author/show/6433082.S_R_Grey

Follow S.R. Grey on Instagram:
instagram.com/authorsrgrey#

Read the first chapter of Exposed: Laid Bare, volume one in S.R. Grey's new erotic romance/paranormal series...

Exposed: Laid Bare (Volume 1)

Chapter One

JUST AS I was taking in a sweeping gaze of the most magnificent Christmas party I'd ever attended, someone snuck up behind me and whispered in my ear, "You are such a little bitch, Dahlia."

"Veronica," I huffed, annoyed.

I tried to spin around to confront my verbal assailant—who also happened to be my best friend and cousin who delighted in driving me crazy—but before I could get my bearings, Veronica's delicate, slender fingers slid over my eyes.

Everything went black, but the smells and sounds of the holidays were still all around me. Eggnog and cinnamon scents punctuated the air, and the comforting lull of classic holiday tunes filled my ears. But with my sight obscured as it was, there would be no more gazing at the yards and yards of multi-colored, twinkling lights draped from the raw wood beam rafters above me, and no more admiring the sparkling, decorated fifteen-foot fir in the far corner of the large banquet hall the party was being held in.

Prior to Veronica's interruption, I'd been mesmerized by the tree with its shiny glass ornaments and bright lights adorning the branches. I found it amazing how the holiday glow made all the beautiful party guests look even more dazzling. Glamorous and sophisticated, all dressed in their holiday party finest and milling around, drinking too much champagne, having too much fun. But the glitz and glamour were momentarily hidden from me, thanks to Veronica's hand over my eyes.

"Are you done," I inquired. I made my tone sound miffed, but I wasn't, not really.

"No, and don't look now," she replied from behind me, hand still in place.

"As if I could," I interjected as I shifted from one way-too-high stiletto heel to the other. "So, why am I a bitch?" I continued. "And why in God's name are you still covering my eyes?"

"First, you're not really a bitch," Veronica replied apologetically. "And secondly, the answer to your other question, my dear, just walked in the door."

Aha! Her answer, not to mention her tone, meant one thing and one thing only—*he* was here.

Oh, boy.

I pushed Veronica's hand away, blinked twice, and peered through the crowd. It wasn't hard to spot the man I sought, not with his commanding height and his room-filling presence. He radiated confidence and outshined even the loveliest of guests. With his coal-black hair and, seemingly, even darker eyes, combined with a lithe body and the best bone structure I'd ever seen on a man, Lucien Chambers was quite the male specimen. Still, I could barely believe what was so clearly in front of me—Mr. Chambers, guest of honor at this year's Lucent Magazine bigwig holiday party, had actually taken it upon himself to grace everyone with his presence.

Interesting.

Lucien, entrepreneur, millionaire at age twenty-four—*multi-millionaire* three years later—was successful and loaded. And at age twenty-nine, as of last month, he'd been declared Chicago's most eligible bachelor.

Well, he definitely deserved the title. Lucien was rich, stunning to look at, and available. I'd previously read that he dated frequently—usually beautiful models, of course—but he'd never gotten married. Perhaps he'd just never found the right one.

No surprise there. I imagined a man such as Lucien would possess rather discerning tastes.

Glancing over at my beautiful cousin, I thought about how Veronica would have been a good match for Lucien. With platinum blonde hair that flowed to her waist, a killer body, and icy blue eyes, she was almost as stunning as Lucien…almost. Oh well. Too bad she was engaged.

I returned my attention back to the situation at hand, murmuring, "Hmm, this *is* unusual."

"What?" I could feel Veronica's cool blue eyes on me, assessing.

"Nobody thought Mr. Chambers would put in an appearance tonight, given his reclusive nature."

"Well, he's here," she replied matter-of-factly.

Yes, he sure was. And—uh-oh—he was currently walking my

way.

"Shit," I hissed rather loudly.

Veronica paid me no heed, though. She was too busy leaning into me and whispering in my ear, "Oh, Dahl, just look at him. That man is so damn sexy."

"I am looking," I said.

And, oh, was I ever. It was almost impossible not to stare, as Lucien was one smoking hot man. And tonight he looked especially magnificent in his dark gray suit, the ritzy fabric allowing his body to move elegantly and fluidly.

"Wow," I sighed. "He is impressive, right?"

"For sure," Veronica murmured.

There was something more about the man, though, something beyond his great looks that made him so appealing. Lucien was a man with great confidence.

Conversely, I was the exact opposite—a woman with very little confidence.

So, of course, as he neared me, I spun around and grabbed up Veronica's hand. "Quick," I said, "let's get out of here."

"What? Why? Are you crazy?" was Veronica's certainly understandable response. She tried to twist away, but I kept my hold firm.

"Come on," I urged once more, this time tugging for effect. "Please, V."

Veronica held steady, but her voice turned soft and understanding when she said, "Why don't you want to meet him tonight, Dahlia? You'll be working with the man soon enough."

"That's exactly why I don't want to meet him," I replied.

I tugged Veronica's arm again to get her moving, and added, "You know my rules."

Finally, *that* got her moving. And just in time, as Lucien was gaining ground.

"Okay, okay," Veronica said as I turned us away at the same second Lucien's searing gaze connected with mine.

Too late, I'm outta here, my parting glance conveyed.

As I dragged my cousin in the direction of the rest rooms— surely a safe spot—she murmured under her breath, "How could I have forgotten about you and your weird idiosyncrasies?"

Okay, yes, she had a point. I was a little weird about my work, quirky even, but my weirdness kept my creativity at play. I am a photographer, you see, and a damn good one. Not meeting my subjects before taking their picture is an integral part of my creative process. I prefer to go in to photo shoots cold. That way I learn my subject as I work. It makes for a better outcome, and I have the award-winning photographs to prove it.

"Come on," I hurried my cousin along, toward an alcove with a tastefully small, gold plate engraved with the word *Ladies*.

"Calm down," she said. "He's not following us now. He stopped to talk with someone."

"He may catch up," I replied, worried.

"Oh, Dahlia…" Veronica shook her head.

She was sweet to indulge me, but she understood my idiosyncrasies. Veronica is a photographer too, and has her own quirks to contend with. The two of us freelance around the city. My cousin is good, very talented, but I am better. Not to brag, it just is what it is. That's why I was awarded the prestigious gig of shooting Lucien Chambers the day after Christmas.

Interacting with him in seven more days would be soon enough. I'd have time to build up my courage by then and, hopefully, not make a fool of myself. Photographing Mr.

Chambers—for a piece Lucent Magazine was running on him and his many business successes—had the power to make or break my career. He gave so few interviews and rarely allowed himself to be photographed, so this was a coup. The only reason he agreed to this news piece was because he'd recently bought a stake in the magazine.

Needless to say, I was nervous as hell. I could not screw up this job.

"I still can't believe you're passing up the chance to meet Lucien Chambers," Veronica mused out loud. "Surely, a little preview won't mess with your wacky ways."

"I'll meet him next week at the shoot," I maintained, keeping Veronica moving through the crowd and away from Mr. Eligible Bachelor.

Finally, we reached the ladies room. I hurried in, Veronica in tow, and closed the door behind us.

Turning to me, Veronica rolled her eyes. "Well, you're safe now. I doubt he'll dare step in here." She gestured around at all the feminine décor in the ornate facility. "There is way too much estrogen in this room for any man."

"I think you're right," I agreed, smiling at all the flowery and frilly detail everywhere.

Stepping over to one of the many floor-to-ceiling mirrors on the walls, I let out a sigh of relief.

But when I took in my reflection—seeing only disheveled auburn hair and green eyes with lashes in dire need of a mascara touch-up—I murmured dejectedly, "Damn, I'm glad he didn't catch up to us. Ugh. Look at me, Veronica, I'm a mess."

"Oh, you're fine," she said.

But, quietly, after a beat, I disagreed and added, "No wonder

I've never had a boyfriend."

My cousin stepped over to me and leaned her head against my shoulder. Lovingly, she adjusted the ruby red spaghetti strap of my silk dress. "You look beautiful, as always, Dahl. Any man would be lucky to have you."

"Maybe," I mused, leaning my head to hers. "Too bad no man wants me."

"That's not true."

"Yeah, it kind of is."

Veronica sighed. "You're gorgeous, hon, but you are a little too picky for your own good."

Now, it was my turn to sigh, because, sadly, she was correct. I was mighty choosy. A few dates, a couple of vanilla kisses. That was my experience in the areas of love, lust, and men. And it was all because my standards were pretty much unattainable.

Not that I had any standards defined, not exactly. Still, it was as if there was this little voice in my head urging me to wait.

I was waiting for something…or someone. I just didn't know which one. In any case, I sure hoped that that something—or someone—happened soon.

Mostly because being a virgin at the age of twenty-six was beginning to feel downright embarrassing.

www.ingramcontent.com/pod-product-compliance
Lightning Source LLC
Chambersburg PA
CBHW060921250626
47159CB00008B/3110